JIM HAS

CW00592113

CORCHO BLISS

Take a wanted gunman; and a hard-drinking penny-pinching gunrunner; and the gunrunner's buxom daughter. And then put them together as a team to sell machine guns to an army of Mexican bandits (or insurgents, depending on your point of view). Fine, unless the army happens to be led by a certain General Lara whose hobbies include holding up trains, sacking towns and hanging his captives. Oh, and one or two other things into the bargain. Such as making life difficult for gunrunners, and trying to take advantage of their daughters.

Wild and delightful . . . Very funny and entertaining from start to finish'

Publishers Weekly

Corcho Bliss

Austin Olsen

CORONET BOOKS
Hodder Paperbacks Ltd., London

For Pat

Copyright © 1972 by Austin Olsen
First published in Great Britain by
Barrie & Jenkins Limited
Coronet edition 1975

The characters and situations in this book are entirely imaginary and bear no relation to any real person or actual happening.

This book is sold subject to the condition that it shall not, by way of trade or otherwise, be lent, re-sold, hired out or otherwise circulated without the publisher's prior consent in any form of binding or cover other than that in which this is published and without a similar condition including this condition being imposed on the subsequent purchaser.

Printed and bound in Great Britain for
Coronet Books, Hodder Paperbacks Ltd,
St. Paul's House, Warwick Lane,
London, EC4P 4AH
by Hunt Barnard Printing Ltd,
Aylesbury, Bucks.

ISBN 0 340 19680 7

He was the only man I ever knew who strapped a grenade inside his crotch, next to his long winter underwear. Come to think of it, he was the only man I ever met in Mexico who wore long winter underwear. Of course there was a reason – not for the underwear – for the grenade. In 1911 it was a lucky man that was allowed the formality of a cigarette before he was shot. However, being a civilised people, the Constitucionalistas or the Federalistas or whoever was momentarily on top would always permit a man a last pee.

Willy was sober when I first met him. He had just slid through one of the batwing doors without disturbing the other. Batwing doors in cantinas are made for men to swagger through – or be thrown out of. Willy opened one half door gently, poked his sharp nose and cold luminous blue eyes through, and, after half a dozen snapshotlike glances around the bar, edged through slowly, swinging just the one half door open.

That's the way I first remember him. A railbird of a man, picking his way into a bar, and then hopping by the clusters of men up to the mahogany bar. He stood above the water trough, both feet on the brass rail so as to get his elbows over the bar. I got him into focus, blinked and belched. I put my chin on my chest to see him. He was that short.

'You always slip into a bar like that, friend?' I asked.

'Thank you,' he said, 'I'll have whiskey. American bourbon, please.'

I rubbed my forehead with the bar rag and tried again.

'The drink's on me. Now, do you always grease into a bar sideways like that?'

He turned his eyes on me. The light from the clear blue eyes warmed my cheeks.

'Sir, you are observant. An unusual man who notices detail. That detail that tells the intelligent observer a whole story. You have deduced that I am a man accustomed to intimate European bars frequented only by rich and wealthy titled noblemen. Those bars have only one door – usually paneled.'

'That so?'

'The same, thank you.' The barkeep poured him another whiskey. 'Yes, my astute friend, any establishment serving alcoholic drinks must be approached gently' – he stopped long enough to throw down his shot – 'unless you are a man of violence.' His eyebrows arched in question.

'No,' I said. It was true. I never have liked violence. The only reason I carried the Bisley Colt on my hip, the two-barreled Remington .41 in a coat pocket and the short-bladed bowie under my left arm was to avoid violence. And I had been violated very few times at this point.

'I said the same thing to myself as I saw you. There is a fine figure of a man. Well over six feet tall. Two hundred pounds of muscle. Arms as big as my legs. The flat green eyes of a gunfighter. But,' he said triumphantly, 'back of those eyes is the soft and gentle heart of a man who hates violence. You, sir, are a man who would kill, if necessary, to prevent violence.'

I just couldn't help myself. The man could speak. Then, too, I had put away a bottle of bourbon and was feeling emotional. I cheered. A miner next to me said something nasty in Spanish. I guess I must have thrown him out of the window because I remembered later, in jail, the glass breaking. However, and it was really a tribute to the oratory of Willy, I had tried to throw the miner not through the tempting window but through the swinging doors. That was my last recollection before I edged my way from painful blackness to an even more painful and God-awful white light. It was while I was still easing my eyes open and gently moving my head that the jail door banging set off the popcorn in my head. It was still popping when I made out a short, shivery man. It was Willy.

'May I present myself?'

I nodded once, but it hurt, so I stopped. Willy went on anyhow. I guess he hadn't really wanted my permission.

'I, sir, am William Harrison Harper the Third.' He bowed slightly. Anyone that drinks a lot can tell when a man is about to throw up. I was just about there and Willy jumped back.

'Look, Mr. William the Third, I am not well, and I am maybe a bit meaner than sometimes, so – '

'Call me Willy,' he said. 'Friend, you have been the victim of a conspiracy,' he said, nodding his head gravely, all sympathy.

I held mine with hands that had grown thick and insensitive. I tried to talk but something closer to a meow came out.

Willy nodded again, then whipped out a cold bottle of beer from under his coat. He had fitted it into an inside pocket. I pulled the cork with my teeth and, without taking the bottle from my lips, drank the whole pint.

The world slowed, rocked and leveled out. I looked at Willy with affection. 'Call me Floyd,' I said. 'Floyd Wheatley.'

Floyd was my uncle's name and Wheatley was from my mother's side of the family.

'Now, my boy,' Willy Harper said, 'I propose to befriend you. Inasmuch as you were genteel enough to invite me to a libation yesterday, I have, in this time of need, named myself as your benefactor.'

'Professor,' I said, 'if you are talking about a drink, there was maybe a half dozen. If, on the other hand, I bought you a libation, I hope you take good care of her. They ain't easy to come by here in Tres Gaviotas.'

'Just so, my poor beset-upon friend. There is a lack of spiritual qualities. A sad want of decent, trustworthy people.'

'Yeah. I guess so. You got something on your mind, Professor?' I asked.

'That depends. You have demonstrated your abhorrence of violence most graphically. However, if I may ask, are you adept with that low-hammered Bisley Colt you were wearing at the time the bartender hit you?'

'Oho,' I said, 'so that was it. A blackjack behind the ear.'

'No, Floyd, he caught you, most uncouthly, I might say, with a bung starter.'

'Yes,' I murmured, mostly to myself, 'I must visit him and help him start a bung or two. I got an idea about the first one.'

'My question concerning the Bisley?'

'Yeah,' I said, 'I can use it. I carried the new swing-out cylinder .45 for a while, but it don't fit my hand right.'

'Still, it is a double action.'

'Yeah. It's a self-cocker all right, but it pulls the barrel off when you don't hammercock the gun. Then I always figure on just one shot anyway.'

'A most professional attitude. Once, before the unfortunate innovation of repeating arms, the basic code of the trained fighting man.' Willy cleared his throat and when he spoke he might have been trying to calm a spooked horse. 'Floyd?'

'Yeah?'

'Were you ever known by the name of Corcho Bliss?' He coughed, then ducked his head as if the question embarrassed him.

One of my saving graces, and utter damnation, has been my reflexes. They seem to operate independent of any thought process. I had his wrist behind his back and his body arched over one knee before he could even cock the derringer. My right arm was crossed over his throat, my left boot pinned his left foot to the floor, and my right knee was bent into the small of his back. I could have killed him as easy as wringing the neck of a dove. He knew it. Sweat stood out on his pale forehead. His eyes widened. But the little cuss held on to his nerve.

'I was just checking your credentials. I need a man like the one that Corcho Bliss was. He's dead, you know.'

I palmed the derringer and sat him down.

'Dead?'

'Buried in El Paso, across the river. It seems there was an altercation and Mr. Bliss received too many .44-caliber loads: forty grains of powder, two hundred grains of lead. An exemplary load, young man, exemplary!'

'Yeah,' I said. 'Much left of his face?'

'No. Not much. Identification was a bit sloppy. However, he was holding a Colt's new service double-action .45-caliber revolver, which Corcho Bliss swore by. The other, uh, participant carried a short-hammered Bisley Colt, similar to yours.'

I held on tight. Maybe I should have cracked his spine. Although if I had I might have missed some of the damnedest things that ever happened to an ex-bandit, actor, gunman and present bum.

'How do you know a .44 hit him?' I asked.

'Well, only one of the .44 cartridges had been fired and he, Corcho Bliss, had been hit twice. And of course, the .45 revolver was next to Bliss. The sheriff pointed this out to the interested bystanders.'

'And . . . ?' I let the question trail off. There was a threat implied. I wasn't much joking either and Willy got my message.

He backed away as he talked. 'Perhaps I should explain my interest,' Willy said. 'I have a business, a highly lucrative one, for a man of my knowledge and contacts. Many of those participating in this cruel revolutionary war, brother against brother, father against father,' he paused and lifted his bright-blue eyes to the ceiling, 'many of these poor benighted souls are killing each other with single-shot weapons.' His head clicked down from its heavenward position and his voice rang with indignation. 'Single-shot weapons, sir!'

'What is your connection?' I was suspicious but still not certain. He might be selling Bibles.

'My connection, sir, is to help the gladiators. To befriend them, without discrimination. Why, I have carloads of fine, slightly used lever-action Winchesters, some of them barreled for smokeless powder. I have cases of better-than-new .44 Colt cowboy pistols. Better than new,' he clarified as my eyebrows raised, 'because,' he said triumphantly, 'they have been tested.'

'Yeah,' I said, 'by Custer at the Little Big Horn, by the whole Sioux nation for a while, and – '

'Of course,' he cut in, 'I do have, in limited number, and at an attractive price, some Colt semiautomatic, smokeless-powder .38-caliber pistols. These develop one-thousand-and-fifty-feet-per-second velocity and will pass through nine one-inch pine boards. I also have a few completely automatic weapons. Machine guns they are called. These are manufactured by Browning, a Utah boy now residing in Belgium, and their rate of fire is frightening. Why, a .30-caliber Colt Browning, model 1895 – '

'I read your sign,' I interrupted. 'What do you want with me?'

'Protection. I often carry great sums of money. A letter of credit in payment of my merchandise is no temptation to brigands, but to expedite sales, I frequently carry up to ten thousand dollars in gold.'

My eyebrows moved again, and he said, 'Yes, I know. More than thirty pounds. I use a double money belt with a shoulder strap under my shirt.' He paused.

'One hundred dollars a month.' He held his palm thrust out to shut off my complaints. 'Plus twenty thousand dollars at the end of our selling trip if I'm still alive. The method of payment stops you from just taking my ten thousand dollars and disappearing.'

'How do I know I'll get the money? That is supposing I get you back alive from your gunrunning trip?' I asked.

'We are not gunrunning,' Willy said. 'We deliver somewhere along the border. We will, however, take orders for firearms. Still, it is a good question. I wouldn't want a dunce working for me. I want you to be absolutely certain about your money. We will go in front of Judge O'Brien in El Paso – '

He stopped as I shook my head slowly, negatively.

'Yes. Well then . . . here in Mexico?'

'Don Hilario Benítez. You will deposit the money with him to be turned over to me, in front of you, reasonably alive, one year from the date we first appear.'

'*¡Hecho!*' he said.

'*¡Hecho!*' I agreed, then said, 'You speak Spanish?'

'Not really,' he said. 'Just expressions like "it's a deal" and a few things like that. I am not really a linguist.'

Hah! Willy could take a figure in English, multiply it in Chinese, add his commission in Greek, and pad it in Spanish, while linguists like me were trying to read the contract. Willy spoke better Spanish than most of the revolutionary generals we finally met.

'All right, Willy. Let's get me out. Advance me my first week's salary and I'll arrange my escape.'

'It's already done,' Willy said. 'I paid twelve dollars for your accommodations, six dollars for your special sleeping arrangements, that, I might explain, was an old saddle blanket. And your fine. That was one dollar. Here are your sixty-one dollars.'

'Hold it. Slow down, hoss. There seems to be some ten dollars floating around somewhere.'

'No.' Willy pursed his lips. 'Ah. I see. You probably didn't count in the cost of your beer.'

'Beer!' I gasped. 'Ten dollars for a beer?'

'That's the price,' Willy said sadly.

'I never pay more than two bits . . . say four bits in a whorehouse.'

'True, true,' he said, 'but how many beers have you bought in this jail?'

He had me there. I held out my hand for the money. I counted it twice and then stuffed it deep down in my pants pocket.

'Willy,' I said, 'I guess I've seen about every way to slice a piece off a peso, but I bet you could show me a couple of new ones.'

I was right, too. On the way out Willy got a ten per cent refund of what he'd paid to get me out. I asked him why and he smiled and said because he'd asked for it.

I shut the jailhouse door just as quick and tight as I could so as not to let any of that prison air out where it might poison some kids or old ladies. Tres Gaviotas was a small town, and Don Hilario lived only two hog wallows and a dead dog from the jail. His house didn't look like much on the outside, but inside it was something. The *mozo* knew me and brought me through the long, dark hall out into the patio. The living room, dining room, Don Hilario's study, and even the bedrooms, all opened on to the patio, which was really a garden with a fountain in the middle. Don Hilario was sitting there sipping sherry wine and reading. He didn't need glasses, and he was as slim as a boy, even if his hair and mustache were all white. His face was brown from the sun and hardly wrinkled. Even so, Don Hilario was pushing eighty. He jumped up and gave me a big *abrazo*, that is a hug and a pat on the back a Mexican gives to say hello if he has not seen someone for a day or so.

'*¿Cómo estás, mi hijo? ¿En qué lío andas?*'

Well, he really did treat me like a son and I was usually in some kind of trouble, so his calling me son and asking about my trouble was natural. When he noticed Willy, he bowed.

'I am your servant, Hilario Benítez Durán.'

Don Hilario knew just about every language, except the Indian tongues along the border, and he said they hadn't written anything so he didn't bother to learn them.

Willy bowed. 'I would be pleased, sir. It *is* sherry, is it not?'

Don Hilario blinked. Then he smiled, clapped his hands, and called for glasses and a bottle.

Willy and Don Hilario sipped their wine, which I could never do, although Willy could sip about as fast as I could drink. I threw mine down and explained to Don Hilario about our deal. Don Hilario called me Floyd all but one time and then he made a joke about the cork out of a wine bottle. *Corcho* is Spanish for cork.

Don Hilario nodded, not in approval, but to show that he understood, while I told him about the $20,000 in gold if we came back together after a year's time.

'Most ingenious. You guarantee your bodyguard's interest in keeping you alive.' He turned to me. 'And you wish to do this?'

'Yeah. I need a new start. You know that place I want.'

'There is one unpleasant possibility,' Don Hilario said. 'Suppose that neither of you returns?'

'In that case you will turn it over to my daughter. She will identify herself with a family photograph.'

'Prudent,' Don Hilario said. 'You are carrying the money?'

'Here you are,' Willy said. He handed Don Hilario a paper.

'What is that?' I asked.

'A letter of credit made out to the bearer for twenty thousand dollars.'

'Here is your change,' I said. I held out the $61.60 that Willy had advanced me.

'Do not be hasty, my boy. Would you prefer my personal check?'

'See you around.' I put on my hat.

'You want the money deposited in cash?'

'Gold,' I said.

'Of course. I know you meant American dollars. And that's what I meant, but a check or a draft is even better, safer –'

'Gold,' I interrupted. 'Hard money. Coin. Fifty-dollar gold pieces. Something like that.'

'Surely you don't expect me to carry, let's see' – Willy's eyes blinked rapidly until he had his cipher – 'some sixty pounds of gold on my person?'

'Nope,' I said.

'Your tracks are deep for a small man.' Don Hilario

pointed the toe of his elegant black shoe at the impression of Willy's boots in the damp grass.

Willy coughed. 'Of course I do carry some gold coins. The nature of my business,' he explained. 'If I may remove my coat and shirt?'

Don Hilario nodded graciously.

Willy laid his coat over a chair. Then his shirt. Over his longjohn underwear, like crossed bandoliers, were money belts. He unbuckled one, then the other. 'I might have a large sum,' Willy said. 'Would you check, Señor Benítez?'

Don Hilario checked all right. Willy had exactly $20,000 in those belts, not a cent more – or less.

After the *mozo* had carted the money away, I said goodbye and started out. Willy fidgeted, then said, 'I should have a receipt.'

'What for?' I said. 'You know how much you gave Don Hilario and so does he.'

'It is not businesslike,' Willy stammered. 'I do not believe in by-passing proper business practices.'

Don Hilario wrote him a receipt in Spanish. Willy read it and said, 'But this states that I cannot collect the money unless Floyd is present,' Willy sputtered, 'or my daughter must present evidence of my death to collect.'

'Yes,' Don Hilario said, 'as long as we are following standard business procedures, I feel it my duty to protect the boy.' He meant me. I was a bit over forty. Willy must not have been more than fifty.

'But,' Willy muttered, 'but . . . suppose I just disappear?'

'That,' Don Hilario said, 'would be most inopportune.'

I got another *abrazo*. 'Goodbye, *vaya con Dios*.'

Outside, Willy said, 'Your friend Don Hilario should practice law.'

'He does.' I grinned. 'On both sides of the border. Tell me, Willy, how come, even with a receipt, you left that twenty thousand dollars in gold with a man you never met before.'

'Why, Floyd, the man's a gentleman. Any fool can see that. Also' – Willy's eyes blinked like the shutters on a signal light – 'I have arranged to deposit the receipt with the Chavez Bank. They will only pay five per cent as they will not be able to use the gold, but they will guarantee my receipt.'

'Willy,' I said, 'let me buy you a drink.'

We left the bar after just the one drink. We were to meet the next morning in front of the train station in Ciudad Juárez. It wasn't far from Tres Gaviotas so I paid off my room and threw my extra shirt and socks into my war bag, rolled it up in a couple of coarse wool blankets and paid four bits American to a water hauler to take me into the big city.

No one knew for sure which way the city would go, Federalista with the 'ins' or revolutionary with the 'outs'. There were two-gunned men walking in pairs all over town. I bought me some soap and a towel, an extra pair of pants and two boxes of .44 Special cartridges. The restaurants were full of hardcases, American and Mexican. I didn't want any new or old friends around me so I bought some dried meat, a few tortillas, the big plate-sized thin wheat ones they make in the North, a couple of *chiles* to give the meat some taste, and took up a couple of beers with me to the Juárez Hotel. There was no room, so I sat in a chair and made tacos with my meat and tortillas and drank the beer. I gave the clerk a quarter and slept in a corner on an old mattress he lugged out for me. I gave him another quarter in the morning for some hot water to shave with. Then I went out to look for Willy. He was there, five minutes before the hour, waiting for me. He gave me the impression that I was late.

I said I was sorry for almost being late and then Willy went on into the Chihuahua train to find us seats. He had the tickets. While he was gone I bought a stack of the big white tortillas, some *chiles* and a lump of barbecued pork. I found an old woman with a clay jar, a *jarro*, filled with water. The water sweats out, evaporates, and keeps the inside cold; there is no better way to have a drink of whiskey than to chase it with some good cold water from a clay *jarro*. She wanted to sell me a new one, but I told her I didn't have time to break it in, to get rid of the green clay taste, so she sold me her old one, at a loss, she said. But then I figured she might have her losses calculated to include a profit, and didn't insist on paying more than she asked.

Just before I swung up on the train, I bought a straw basket and dumped my goods in it. My blanket roll and war bag was already aboard.

I missed Willy the first time. He was sitting next to a beautiful girl. I could tell, of course, that she was no innocent and was probably headed to a high-class house in Chihuahua, or maybe even into Mexico itself, as the Mexicans call their capital city. She whispered in Willy's ear and gave him a hug just as I stopped to speak to Willy. I grinned and winked at him. He raised an eyebrow.

I grinned and winked again. 'I'll pick me a seat up the line. Three's a crowd, I reckon.'

Willy said, 'Sit down, my lad. Sit down! If you need food or drink, I have a supply. Help yourself. I'll give it to you at cost.'

'That go for all the provisions?'

'Yes, my boy. Of course.'

Each end of my grin must have just about met at the back of my head. I turned to look at the girl. She looked away and started fooling with one of those silver-handled mirrors.

She was just about Willy's size, but there wasn't anything skinny about her. She was rounded off nicely. Her hair was up high, showing her ears. They were pink and clean. She had china-doll blue eyes and white teeth but I guess what I looked at most were her boobies. She wore a low-cut dress like the girls at a house will do, and I could have seen her belly button except for a cross she had squeezed down there between them. They were so white I could see the little blue veins. They turned a little pink after a second or so. So did her throat. It was then I lifted up the chain and pulled that cross out so's to see better.

When I came to, they had turned on the gas lamps and I was mixed up a little.

'How bad is it?' I said.

I caught something about 'behind your ear'. My fingers came away sticky with blood. My stomach folded over on itself while my heart raced.

'How about the others?'

'What others?'

'Why, the Deacon and the kid and Curley! Are we still on the train? What went wrong? We got to get off the train!'

I came to my full senses there in the aisle. Willy had me by one arm but his toes were just touching the floor. The girl had my coattails and was hauling hard, but she might have been a kitten playing with my sleeve for all I noticed her.

'Hold on,' I called out. 'I'm all right now. Let's sit a minute.'

We slipped back into our seats. Hardly anyone had noticed the fuss except about thirty people. I felt the welt alongside my head. It was puffy and sore but hardly bleeding at all. The girl was sort of scared-looking so I clapped a hand on her knee, friendly like. 'Don't you worry none, honey, I'll be all right.'

'No, you won't. You put one of those big freckled paws on me once more and I won't hit you with a mirror; I'll put a forty-one-hundredths-of-an-inch hole in your belly. Yes, I will. Amen. I will!'

I snatched my hand back. She was the most touchy thing.

'Look,' I explained, and patiently, too, 'I meant to pay. I'm not a guy that feels a girl's boobies and then backs out when he hears the price. I'm ready to go all the way.'

The click stopped me. There just is not one other thing so short and yet so authoritative as the click that a .41 Remington makes being cocked.

'Apologies. Apologies. Whatever.' I was getting a little tired of this girl. I pulled out my hideaway pint and took a quick but solid shot. 'In a minute,' I said, 'just as soon as my head and me make an arrangement, I will find another seat. My apologies.'

I took another deep drink. The liquor went down smooth and stayed in my stomach, warm. I poured a cupful of cold water from the *jarro* to chase the whiskey with. The girl swallowed hard, but looked away when I caught her watching me drink.

'Willy,' I said, 'what you got your water in?'

'A metal canteen, my lad. Unbreakable it is, and holds a quart – '

'A quart of gagging hot water,' the girl interrupted.

'Now, my dear,' Willy said, 'there is a lot to be said for warm water.'

'Name something,' she said.

'Well, it does not hunt out a dental cavity the way cold water does.'

'And you can wash stockings in it.' She turned to me. 'Say, is that water cold?'

'Why, ah, yes, Miss . . . uh?'

'My name is Pearl Harper.' She held out a traveling cup made out of telescoping tin tubes.

'Harper! Why,' I said, 'you're Willy's wife! The old goat!' I was more than surprised. Downright shocked. The old lecher. I poured her cup full, and when she said, 'No, I am the old goat's daughter,' I kept right on pouring. Even after she pulled her patent telescoping drinking cup back out of the way.

I woke up late. I looked back to see Willy and his daughter, Pearl, asleep. At least I guessed she was asleep. Willy's face was buried under his *sarape* and I could guess where his mouth was by the way the sarape would bellow up and then settle down. I could almost see the fumes flicker up past the gaslight and explode. He snored the way an off-gaited horse trots.

A train ride used to be a big thing with me back when I was a kid on a homestead in Utah. Our place was maybe three miles from town and I would hear that lonesome whistle calling late at night. That whistle and the stars shining down through that attic window would just half wake me. As the Deacon used to say, I'd get dreamy on a train. He swore that once, in the middle of a job, I sat down and got so dreamy that he took my watch and fifty dollars before he realised it was me.

Still, and there is not a bit of use in denying it, I like trains. Cinders and ash, heat and cold and all. It beats riding an ornery, obstinate and contrary brute of a horse. I'm not like some men that spend a lot of time in the saddle and, because of that, can't stand horseflesh. I don't mind it a bit. As a matter of fact, a good smart two- or three-year-old tastes almost like beef. Now you might not be able to eat a train, but it won't bite you or kick you or wind-break itself or get itself lost. I'll take a train, cinders and all, for traveling, anytime.

I pulled out a pair of moccasins I had some Reservation Utes make for me once and slipped them on. They beat boots for traveling, although I made a mistake once and wore them in a fight. I busted my big toe kicking a Texas editor in the head. Lucky I didn't catch him straight on or I might have lost the foot. Although even a boot won't help too much in that case, still you can keep the damage down and maybe even get an idea into his head. It's the only way.

Once I got my moccasins on I walked on down through our car, past the soldiers asleep on the rear seats, into the next and last car. Like always, the drinkers and the card players had rigged up a table and turned a seat around so that the players could keep tabs on each other.

They didn't stand a chance of hearing me. I lived with the Utes for a while and can walk on dried cotton-ball pods without you hear me, let alone in a train with its rattling and roaring. So I just stood back a ways and watched.

One, facing me, was maybe twenty years old and shouldn't have run off and left his mother. His hair was long and wispy and he kept blowing it out of his soft blue eyes. He was studying his down card which I figure for a five. He had two fives and a seven showing. He bet ten dollars, gold, into a pair of sixes. He just had to have that five in the hole. The man with the sixes didn't actually cheer, but he did not break into tears when the boy bet, and I figured he was holding three sixes to the kid's three fives.

'I'll just call that,' he says. He was a big fat man. He was hairy, too. His hair just missed taking in his eyebrows and his eyebrows were not much bigger than his mustache, which could have been a good place for a hide-out gun. On top of this, his hair was bright red. His skin, what you could see of it, was about the color of his hair. He was chewing tobacco. He was easily as big as me and a sight uglier. 'Call and raise fifty,' he said.

He held up his chips and dropped four tens – blues – in. The kid looked worried. The man with his back to me spoke then and I had to lean forward to hear him say, 'Put in the other chip.'

'What?' Red grunted.

'Just a ten-dollar chip. An oversight.' A soft voice, but I tagged that gent as one to take into account.

'Shore,' Red roared, 'what's ten bucks to Old Riverboat Charley.'

The gent with his back to me nodded and then turned his up card over, folding.

The kid pushed in four more gold pieces. He was losing all right. The losers play with money and the winners use chips.

The kid caught another five. Red picked up another four. The kid showed two pair, fives and sevens against sixes and fours. The kid was already counting out his money to bet before Red even got his card.

'Goddamn a pup that plays poker. Never knows enough to get out of a hand. Beat on the board, by God.'

'Exactly,' the man with his back to me whispered. 'Beat on the board and the fool stayed.'

'That's what I said,' Red growled. It took him a minute before he caught on. 'Look, here, tinhorn, you ain't even in this game, so keep your mouth shut.'

'No,' Whisperer said, 'I ain't. However, I will allow myself the privilege of commenting on the players, once they have commented themselves. Now,' he went on in the same quiet, hoarse voice, 'if you don't like it, why you can take your chips and stuff them up your lard ass.'

'Goddamn you!' Red pushed his chair back.

'Fives and sevens bet,' the Whisperer said dispassionately.

'Well, now.' Red grinned. 'I guess you talk, kid. Bet your hand.'

The kid studied his hole card. He had sevens and fives up against Red's sixes and fours. He finally shoved out his stack. A real greenhorn. If you are losing, bet more. That way you can lose more, faster.

Red chuckled. He counted out a hundred and ten dollars, which was what the kid has thrown in.

'And I'll raise you another hundred.'

'Now,' Whisperer said, 'we said table stakes.'

The voice was strange to me, but there was a way he had of picking his words and, by now, even the back of his head was beginning to pick at my memory like I do at a bit of meat stuck between my teeth.

'Okay,' Red said, 'but if the kid wants to dig, it's okay with me.' He guffawed.

'Okay,' the kid said, an edge on his voice, 'I'll dig.' He pulled out a coin purse and sat it on the table. 'There's five hundred in there, big man. You got any money or is your mouth the only big thing about you?'

The Whisperer chuckled. 'He sure called the turn,' he said. Then he spoke to the kid. 'You got guts, stranger.'

Red's jaw dropped. Then his eyes narrowed and he ripped a purse out from his pants pocket and counted out ten fifty-dollar gold pieces. 'There, baby!' He flipped over his bottom card and he had them. Three sixes and two fours. No wonder he didn't believe the kid.

Red snorted, then grinned. 'Well, kid, easy come, easy go.' He reached out for the pile.

I moved back and away to the wall.

'You got the manners of a pig,' the kid said. 'Keep your shitty hands off my pot.'

The kid didn't look quite so young nor anywhere as innocent as he had. He flipped over a seven to show sevens over fives.

Red's eyes bulbed. He shook his head. He tried talking but he just stuttered. Then he looked at the Whisperer, back at the kid and again at the Whisperer.

'You bastards. You cheating sons of bitches.'

He was right, too. The cards were too pat. Two cardsharps taking a big man for a lot of money.

'You want to take him, stranger? Or should I? I assume, lard ass, that you were talking to me.' The Whisperer put a foot against Red's chair, so's he couldn't get out. I saw his shoulder slump and knew his fingers were touching a gun.

'Not unless you don't want him,' the kid said. 'Can't get a rep shooting shitheads.'

'All right. The game is open. One .45 to open. Draw or get the hell out.' The Whisperer might have been talking about a game of draw poker for all the emphasis he put on the words.

'I ain't got a gun.' Red's voice was small. He was looking at death and he knew it. 'I apologise. Sorry. All the money I had. Excuse me.'

He stood up slowly, turned and backed away, then with all the will power a man could want, he turned his back and slowly, slowly walked out.

'Let him go,' I said.

'What?' The kid's head jerked around.

'Easy, kid,' the Whisperer said. 'Sit down, Corcho. I heard you clomp up. Wondered how long you'd stand there.'

Clomp up. He had ears all right, but better than ears he was wearing a flasher, a ring with a mirror in the bottom so as to see the cards you deal, or don't deal. He guarded his back with it, too.

I sat to the right of the kid and to the left of the Whisperer.

'Hello, Gene. What happened to your voice?'

'Don't really know. It was all right though until some girl tried to kill a man that laid her and then walked out without paying. I got in the way.'

'Yeah,' I said. 'Did she ever get her money from you?'

His eyebrows drew down and veed. So did his mouth. There were times when I have seen that long, ugly horsy face in my nightmares. He's the only man I was ever afraid of who did not have a gun on me. Gene scared me so bad that when I was with him I had to make a show of how brave I was. Gene had a lot of names, and like me, he was dead now. Gene and Corcho. I laughed. Then he did, too. He just exploded. He couldn't stop.

The kid looked at me, rubbing his Adam's apple.

'I never seen nobody could talk like that to Gene,' he said. 'Not nobody. He ain't never laughed much before, neither.'

'Corcho doesn't do it too often either,' Gene said.

'Corcho?' the kid said. 'That's cork. What you called "Cork" for?'

'Corcho,' I said, and before Gene could say more, I said, 'Corcho is just a nickname. Call me Floyd, Floyd Wheatley.'

Gene nodded as if he liked my last name. 'And my name is Gene Harrison.'

We shook hands.

'What is this?' the kid asked. 'Didn't you ever know your last names before?'

'No, what's in a name?' Gene said. 'A Floyd by any other name would smell' – he wrinkled his nose – 'the same.'

'Well,' the kid said, 'I never heard of any Corcho before anyway.'

'Only through ignorance, kid,' Gene said. 'You would be surprised how many people don't know anything about anyone who hasn't been on the stage or with one of the circuses.'

'Like Wild Bill,' the kid said knowingly.

'Yeah,' I said. 'The only thing was he always wanted to kiss and hold hands.'

That broke Gene up and he went to haw-hawing again. He had a couple of red spots in his cheeks and he looked almost alive.

The kid was a little put out at Gene laughing.

'I guess you don't know me, but up around New Mexico I got myself a reputation.' The way he said 'reputation', it was four words.

'You sure do remind me of someone,' I said.

'Yeah? Who?'

I shook my head a little. I puckered up my lips and was going to scratch my head but I didn't want to overact. Fact is I had been on the stage, just like Wild Bill, only he never got the hang of it and I was getting pretty good until they brought up an old warrant for me.

'Say,' I said, 'you're left-handed.'

'Yeah, I sure am,' he crowed.

'No. I reckon not. For a minute, I thought maybe it was Bonney. You look like the Kid but he wasn't left-handed.'

'He sure was.'

'A whole lot of people think that, but I knew Billy and liked him, too. I mean the only way he ever hurt people was to kill them. No, kid, *the* Kid was not left-handed.'

'Care to bet on that?' he said, tight-lipped.

'Maybe, but how can you prove I'm wrong?'

'Never mind. Let Gene hold the stakes and he can decide who's right.'

'Fair enough.'

'How about ten dollars?' I said.

'How about a thousand?' he said.

'Gene,' I said, 'there seems to be a difference in our thinking on this bet.'

'I never knew the other Kid, but I wouldn't bet into this one too hard. He is not a true gambler.'

'Well,' I said, 'it don't really matter. I got about sixty dollars and that's her.'

'Put it up,' the kid said.

'In my own good time, if you please!'

Gene stared at me, mouth open, and then he was off again. I mean he laughed. Gene was an educated man, college and Greek and all, and sometimes, drunk, he'd talk just like an actor except he made it up by himself.

'Slow down,' I says, 'I guess you didn't hear about my schooling. Someone thought with a good disguise on I would look like a bandit, so I worked in some plays. One was called *The Wild Bunch and the Lady*, or *The Honor of a Desperado.* I learned a few real fancy speeches, read all the plays, too. I read some we didn't even put on.'

'Put up the sixty,' the kid said. He didn't much care about my life in the theater.

'Don't rightly like to take a boy's money. Do you think it's all right, Gene?'

' "Neither a borrower, nor a lender be," ' Gene said. 'However, our greatest poet made no mention of gambling, so I would assume that a wager is in order.'

'Huh?' the kid said.

'He means we should bet. Here.' I handed over my sixty.

The kid was so busy sorting through his war bag that he just couldn't see my money there on the table.

'Put it up, kid,' Gene said.

'What, Gene? Oh, sure. The money. Here it is. Sixty dollars about to breed.' He laughed pretty hard at his humor. I didn't bother to grin and Gene just grunted.

The kid fished an envelope out of the mess he yanked out of his canvas war bag and then took an old photograph out of the envelope. It was so old that it was yellow at the edges. I had seen that same picture a dozen times.

'I wish I could pick up sixty dollars this easy every day.' He jabbed that old tintype at me and whinnied. 'I got you fucked. This here's Billy the Kid and that pistol that he's packing is on his left side. So's his rifle!'

He cackled a little and handed the picture over to Gene. Gene looked at it and shook his head a trifle. 'Looks like the kid's right. He got you with your pants down and a good hold on that short hair.' That was Gene. He'd talk just as nice and pretty as you might want and then he'd come out like any drunken cowhand.

'Gimme my money, Gene,' the kid crowed.

'Could I see that photograph?' I acted as if I hadn't seen it before.

'Wait a minute. I won. Now gimme the money. Gene!' His voice had tightened up until he could have been a castrated screech owl. 'You gimme that money or I'll shoot you, you son of a bitch, you.'

'Hold on, kid,' I said. 'Could I make just one more bet?'

'What kind of a bet?' He was spoiling for trouble. I could have used his snotty voice to play villains during my year at the 'profession'.

'A simple one. I'll just bet that I can shoot you through your pretty little mouth before you can get your gun out of its pretty little holster. Gene can hold stakes, and if I don't quite make it, we'll send the money to your mother, if you got one, which I doubt.'

'You can't talk to me that way.'

'Reach!' I said.

'You sure do joke.' The kid laughed the same way that a cowhand laughs when the ramrod tells him the same joke he told the ramrod the night before. 'Here's the picture. I guess a guy can forget about a man's gun hand after so many years. Why, you were probably a lot younger then.'

'Yes,' I snapped, 'but a whole lot smarter than you might get to be if you should live to be twice as old as I am.'

'Hadn't you better look at the photograph while your eyes are still good?' Gene said. Then he was at it again. He sounded like a girl when he laughed. And he ended up in a fit of coughing. Still I guess he didn't laugh too much and he couldn't shoot people as often as he once had. So I figured that gambling and an occasional laugh was about all he got out of life now.

I held up the photograph so that they could both see it. 'I learned about this from an expert. Somebody took this print off the wrong side of the plate. Look at the buttons on his vest and his shirt. Men's buttons are always on the right side. These are on the left. Anyway, Pat Garrett told me that when he shot Billy, the Kid had a butcher knife in his left hand and his revolver in his right.'

'I don't know about that, but I don't savvy the buttons.'

'My buttons on this shirt are on the right-hand side, so are the buttons on my coat and pants. So are yours and Gene's. In this old picture the buttons are cn the *left* side.'

Gene just nodded his head. He got it right away.

'Hell, that don't prove anything. Look. You can see he's got the gun on his left side.'

I held the photo up wrong side against the window. The sun, just now coming up in the east, was bright. 'Look, if you see this photograph wrong side to, which side's his gun on?'

'The right,' the kid said, 'but it's on his left on the other side, the right side.'

'Gene,' I said, 'I give up. Who wins? That's all. You just say.'

'You do, Corcho.'

Just then the train stopped. The locked wheels screamed and everything not fastened to the floor tried to get up front, into the engineer's cabin. That included Gene, the kid and me. About the time I got unstuck from a wall and fell down on top of, I believe, the kid, I caught a boot, Gene's, I think, and decided to rest a while. When I got all rested I opened my eyes and looked around a bit, but without moving my head. What with bandits, revolutionaries and Federales any unexpected stop might be fatal and I wasn't interested in attracting any attention.

The first thing I saw, about six feet away from me, was Gene. He was grinning up at something on the other side of the ceiling. He was dead. There were eight or nine more bodies flung along the aisles. None of them was the kid. I eased up and looked out a window. The sun was almost up, but it was cold and men wrapped in *sarapes* were standing around fires. They all had rifles of some kind slung over their shoulders, muzzle down. They were dressed like any bunch of bandits, so they couldn't be Federal troops there in Chihuahua; they had to be either out-and-out bandits or General Lara's part-time revolutionary troops.

The passengers stood in a group off to one side. I felt better when I saw Willy and his daughter, Pearl, with them. There were a few soldiers guarding them, but they weren't overdoing it and I figured that there was something special on the train that they wanted. I wasn't wrong either, for just then a man was shoved from the next car just down from where I watched. He fell to his knees, slowly got to his feet and then proceeded to use beautifully enunciated Spanish to blister those armed men. What he said in Spanish came out something like this in English, although English isn't much for cussing and he was pretty mad and, even for a Mexican, his tongue was educated. Anyway, he said:

'You two sons of whores whose mothers were whores and their mothers whores have dared to touch General Agustín Bernal y López.'

He took a breath and I figured that he was really going to tear into them when a thick man on a buckskin horse rode up. He leaned over to look down into the general's face when he spoke.

'How are you, General Traitor? How is my General Judas?' It was Lara all right, General Lara.

His voice was just as thick and stubborn as his body. I knew that General Bernal y López was a dead man. The

General knew it, too. Still, as the Mexicans say, he had plenty of pants.

'General Lara, I wrote you my reasons for leaving the division and it was not for cowardice as you well know. Nor have I betrayed you. How many know of the tower? Just the three of us. I could have told, yet I was silent. And even you . . . yes, General Lara, you too. I could have led them to you had I so wanted. Now I want only to be left alone. I will settle my affairs in Chihuahua and return to El Paso, never again to live in Mexico. I will die among the gringos so that your division will be your division, and not be split by fights between Pablo González and myself.'

'Coronel González did not desert,' Lara said.

'Pablo has no moral courage.'

'And my fine-tongued general who deserted me has courage. He also knows where the tower is. We know. You, my schoolteacher general; Pablo the Butcher; and me, Lara the Bandit. We three know.'

'Did you stop this train for me?' General Bernal y López asked.

'Yes,' Lara said. 'You.'

'Because I deserted or because of the tower?'

The shot rang out. Horses jumped. Half of the passengers went to their knees. I reached for my Bisley. It was gone.

General Bernal y López had his mouth open and I was sure he had been about to say something about the tower. He never would. Lara got him through the chest, so close that his coat was smoldering from the powder's flash.

Lara turned his big bay horse towards the line of horsemen. He called out to them, his voice booming through the clear desert air.

'General Bernal y López, a brave and wise man, followed General Lara into many battles. He was an educated man. He could read, and write, too.' He removed his sombrero. You could have hidden a couple of ten-gallon cowboy hats in it. 'He overstayed his leave, but in the end he came back. Nobody leaves Lara. Never! May his soul rest in peace.'

He jammed his sombrero on his head and reined his big

bay over towards the prisoners. The horse picked its way delicately over General Bernal y López's body and stopped in front of the prisoners.

An officer trotted up.

'At your orders, *mi general.*'

'First the soldiers. How many Federalistas?'

'There were about forty, *mi general.*'

'*¡Chinga tu madre, cabrón!*' Lara was not very polite. 'When I ask you a question, answer it.'

That officer, by his color, must have been about three-quarters Indian, but he was a whole lot lighter than Willy Harper's daughter, Pearl, when he answered.

'*Mi general*, there are six who are live enough to question.'

'Bring them here!'

In a minute they were lined up in front of Lara. The first man, a sergeant, was still bleeding from a head wound, but he stood straight and looked right at Lara.

'We got a good horse and rifle for you. You keep your rank. If you can't find a girl in camp, you can have your pick when we take next town. Whatever you find, after the fighting is over, is yours. What do you say?' Lara knew a good man when he saw him.

'No. I have been a sergeant in the Army of the Republic of Mexico for twenty years and I shall keep on being one.'

'Not for long,' Lara said. 'Shoot him.'

They moved him away a bit and a slender youth with big brown eyes shot the sergeant in the back of his head.

The next three volunteered.

The fifth was a young boy. He couldn't have been more than fifteen. His dark curly hair almost covered his ears. He was square-shouldered and slim. He stepped forward and saluted.

'I do not change sides, *mi general.* I am not a general, but neither am I a deserter, nor a Judas, nor a coward.'

Lara, for all his heft, came down out of that saddle the way a bit of white fluff falls from a cottonwood tree. He embraced the boy. Tears must have been in his eyes because you could hear them when he talked.

'It is not the same,' Lara said. 'General Beltrán knew better. He was a wise man. He could read. He could write . . . and he left me . . . now you . . . you are just a boy. You come along with General Lara and help make a new Mexico. You and me. What do you say?'

'No.' The boy's eyes were shining.

General Lara gave him another big hug. Then he stepped back, wiping his eyes on his sleeve and said hoarsely, 'I wish I had a son just like you.' He turned to the officer and, in his normal voice, said, 'Shoot him.'

General Lara swung back up in the saddle. He wanted to see all the prisoners, he said, and I knew that he didn't like to look up to anyone. On that big buckskin, he was as tall as I am. He looked at the group for a minute, then called out in Spanish, for Lara's English was limited to 'son of a bitch', which he used to Americans when he wanted to be polite, 'There is a gunrunner among you. A certain Señor Weely. Please step forward.'

A man who might have been an American, at least his English was border Texas, stepped up and repeated the statement in English.

Lara waited about three seconds. He was an impatient cuss. 'Step forward or be shot.'

The American, looking hardcase, stepped forward and translated, but no one moved except to look at one another. I couldn't see Willy but I bet he was in the back row.

'Shoot him,' Lara said.

'But, my general, how will we know which one to shoot?' the border character asked in fluent but northern-accented Spanish.

'Easy,' Lara said, 'shoot them all.'

He had reined his horse away when Willy called out loudly, his thin piping voice pulling Lara's horse around.

'One moment, my General Lara, Napoleon of the West, Liberator of the Poor, I believe you might mean me. My first name is Willy. Señor Willy Harper, at your orders.'

Lara stared at Willy for a long moment, then he said, 'I

heard of Napoleon. He had a good bunch of boys. Maybe as good as mine?'

Willy pursed his lips. 'In spirit, no, but much better armed. He won his battles due to his extraordinary intelligence, courage, vitality – he looked like you, General Lara – and,' Willy added, 'he had the best arms money could buy.'

I tried to get through to Willy. If ever a man wanted to get a message through a hunk of space without making a sound, it was me. Nobody could swallow that kind of syrup. When Lara spoke, I just froze, not knowing what I could possibly do.

'I think you are right, man. I need better guns. I guess I must be smarter than that *cabrón*, Napoleon, eh, because I been doing pretty well with no-good guns.'

That Willy. He knew people.

'Well,' said Lara, 'you going to buy me some new guns?'

'I would be delighted to act as your agent,' Willy said. 'How many and what kind of arms do you desire?'

The lean, wolfy translator touched Lara's boot and whispered something.

'Right,' Lara said. 'Get a horse for my agent.' He turned to Willy. 'We'll talk a few hours away. The Federalistas will be here soon.'

Willy just nodded and then that touchy blond daughter ran out and cried, 'No! If Willy goes, I go!'

Lara just grinned and said, '*Encantado.*' He liked girls. All kinds. He married them by the dozens. 'Bring another horse,' Lara called.

I took a deep breath of air and let myself out the broken door. 'If you don't mind, General,' I said, 'get another horse.'

The clicks of Winchesters and Colts being cocked sounded like a thousand giant crickets on a warm damp night and I figured that there might be that many firearms of one kind or another aimed at my belly.

Lara's horse danced over.

'Who are you?' he asked.

'I'm his bodyguard,' I said weakly.

'His bodyguard? His bodyguard!' Lara turned to his troops, and as he yelled, he slipped his Colt back in its holster. 'He's his bodyguard!' Lara whooped and spluttered and pounded on his saddle till his buckskin danced. His troops howled, too, and what was even better, they let the hammer down on their guns. I even grinned to show them I could take a joke.

When Lara could talk, he said, 'Bring him a horse.'

Pearl rode alongside Willy when there was room between the spiny *nopales.* She rode astride and her skirts were hiked up enough to show a lot of leg. I guess Lara's men must have figured that she was the general's private stock because one old boy with a face that looked like it had been cut out of dried mesquite pulled in close to her without noticing. He said something over his shoulder to Pearl and then, grinning, turned to look. His sun-wrinkled face crumbled and he almost spurred his horse into a dry wash getting away.

How Pearl took all that riding I don't know. I know I was getting sore around the tail and my rump had to be tougher than hers although she did have me beat for padding. We stopped to blow the horses so I walked mine up to where Willy and Pearl were squeezed into a patch of shade. Willy had his mouth all pursed up like a tightened Bull Durham tobacco pouch. He let his drawstring out enough to snarl 'Bodyguard! You call yourself a bodyguard!'

My mouth was open trying to say something without any help at all from my brain when Pearl said, 'Oh, Willy, shut up. You expect him to fight that killer's whole army?'

'He is being paid handsomely to protect me – us – and I expect the service to match the reward.'

Willy was going to say more, but I put in, 'I wonder who Don Hilario will give that money to?'

That stopped Willy. 'Why should he give it to anyone until a legitimate claim is made?'

'A legitimate claim would be the three of us, all there in

front of Don Hilario, or Pearl with some proof of our death,' I pointed out.

'Correct,' Willy said.

I shook my head. 'I hope Pearl makes it.'

'Lara won't just shoot us down like, like . . . ' Willy sputtered, 'dogs – '

'No,' I said, 'on the other hand you saw how he treats deserters.'

'You mean that old general he shot back at the train?' Pearl asked.

'Yes.'

'But we can't be deserters,' Pearl said. 'We've never joined.'

'As a recently departed friend of mine used to say,' I said, 'that is merely your opinion.'

Pearl just cocked her head at me. Willy looked sad. Then the thin dark gent who had translated some for Lara back by the train spoke up. He must have left his horse down the trail someplace.

'You've joined. All of you. For life, which may not be a very long sentence.' His English was pure Texan. Funny how Texans speak English southern and Spanish northern.

Pearl suddenly didn't look nearly as tough as she did when she pulled that little Remington two-shooter on me in the train.

'Pearl,' I said, 'saying a thing doesn't make it so. One way or another we'll make it back to the other side of the Rio Bravo and we'll be laughing and drinking and – '

'Let's let it stay with the laughing and drinking,' she said weakly.

It did me good to hear Pearl come back like that. Her color was better, too, although you had to look twice to see the edges of a smile.

'Sure,' Tex said, 'when you get back, send me a letter.' He turned to me. 'Of course, that is merely my opinion. You know the Deacon?'

'Knew,' I said. 'He's dead – ' I stopped short. I didn't want anyone connecting me with the Deacon, dead or alive.

'I don't know any preachers. The gent that used to talk like I just said is dead. Died of cerebral jammage back in Las Vegas, New Mexico. Sad affair. Left a wife and four girl friends. Why, that man – '

He cut me off. 'I saw him. I knew Gene. The Deacon.'

He tilted his head and the overhead sun flashed against his blond hair. His nose was sharp, his eyes small, but bright and full of hell even if his dark skin showed no wavy lines, age or experience, either one. He would be a man that knew guns. And maybe knew me too. But where?

'You knew Gene – '

'Let's get out of the sun.' I cut him off before he could say any more. I pulled him along with me away from Willy and Pearl. 'Floyd's my name,' I said. 'Come from cow country up around – '

'El Paso,' he finished for me. 'Long time no see, Corcho.'

I reached and so did he. Except he came up fast, with a gun. I just reached. My holster was mighty empty, along with my hand, and so was my stomach.

When after a year or two of absolute quiet there was no explosion, I let out some air.

'You got a good piece of nerve, and some speed,' I said.

'I knowed you didn't have a gun, but you triggered me, slapping at that damn, silly, empty holster.' His laugh was off pitch and I thought, *'That's a good one. He's scared.'* He tried to roll a cigarette and couldn't so he passed the Bull Durham to me. I made one, but it wouldn't have won any prizes, not even on a dude ranch.

'I sure didn't want to shoot you,' he said. 'If Lara don't shoot me, Pablo will, and you may be my only chance on making it out of this volunteer army . . . alive and' – he looked around quickly – 'rich. Richer than Colonel King. Richer than old man Terraza was before the *revolucionarios* ran off his beef.'

'Congratulations,' I said. 'I like to know rich people.' I edged away. He looked like a man I might have known once. Maybe someone that I should remember. Blond hair. A craggy kind of a face. Maybe a couple of years younger than me. Still, I couldn't fix a place, a time and, even less, a name to his face.

'Hold on,' he said. 'I mean us. You and me. I don't know how much we can take out, but it won't be less than a million.'

Dust was drifting back from moving horses. The men around me began mounting. I got a foot in the stirrup and just before I swung up into the saddle, I said, 'You really knew Gene?'

'I did,' he said. 'He used to talk just like a book, when he wanted. I saw you stop him once, over a card table. In Tombstone.'

'I didn't stop Gene. You got a name?'

'He didn't kill you.' He spurred on past me and said, 'Call me Tex. I'll see you in camp.'

I guess I have known fifty Texes. Anyone that wanders out of Texas could use that nickname. But he had seen Gene and me that time in Tombstone. No wonder I hadn't noticed him then. Gene didn't kill me, as Tex said, but I doubt if I will ever come closer to death without dying nor be as scared again. It was the first time I had ever met a man who did not really much care whether he lived or died.

Although I had just turned twenty-one, I had counted myself a man since the last big Apache uprising when I lost my home and my folks. The only reason they didn't get me was luck, the old .45–70 I had with me (along with over twenty cartridges, for I was on my way home from the trading post when they jumped me), and a certain natural talent for shooting. Besides, I heard later, the hostiles didn't think my horse and rifle were worth risking more than the one brave I shot dead and the other I winged.

They went on after a few minutes of racing around me. I was in a nest of boulders and prickly pears. When I didn't break cover, they shot my horse and, carrying the dead brave with them, rode off.

I didn't budge till dark and then I walked home. I could see the fire glowing long before I got there, then I ran the last few miles. With my lungs about burned up, I stopped, just a rifle shot away.

I hallooed, tears running down my cheeks. No matter how long or hard I called, nobody answered. I finally cocked my rifle and walked over. I was very scared inside and crying with my need to hear my mom cry out to me. But there was only the quiet.

Cold water hit me and the sun was shining. I called out 'Maw . . . Paw . . . Dickie . . . ' then a couple of big hands had me by the shoulder. The big hands gave me a shake that rattled my teeth. I never can remember more than his hands.

'They're dead. Dead and buried, boy. There's the graves.'

I remembered then. A little. I had buried them myself. I could remember putting little Dickie in last and rolling the rocks on over. I never remembered how they looked and I know that if I ever do it will be my death.

After that I sold what I could and took to wandering, turning my hands to whatever. There was always work then. Men died often enough to make plenty of jobs. I worked one summer with an old Canadian prospector. I was the packer, cook and dishwasher, but I learned enough to go out on my own; my working gear was a pick, a shovel and a pan. And little as I knew, I made wages. No one else would go into Apache country. That's where I worked. Still half crazy from losing my folks, I guess.

When I first hit Tombstone, there was no place to stay, except to rent a room at one of the fancy houses by the hour and I couldn't stay long enough to get my boots off at the prices they charged. I had a couple of ounces of gold that I had washed out of five different creeks during almost three months up in the Chiricahua mountains. The Apaches knew I was there and they were looking for me in a halfhearted way. One day a couple of them got close enough to find me. I killed one outright and furrowed a piece of coarse black hair from the other. I meant to kill him too. When he came to he was spread-eagled out, staked hands and feet, looking up at the sun.

I pulled back, away from that Apache, and waited for the sun to hit the canyon rim. I knew no one would be looking for him until the next day. When he saw me, his eyes flashed and he snarled something that I figured must have been an opinion about my character. I squatted, picking my teeth with a splinter, and watched him. His expression slipped for just a second when I drank from my canteen; I knew he must be pretty thirsty, so I had myself another drink.

Then I ran a hitch around a big rock and rolled it in the creek. I pulled his feet down into the water until the water rippled over his belly. By twisting his head he could almost touch the water with his cheek. Almost.

That country in August is dry and hot. I figured he might last a couple of days unless a stray wolf or the buzzards got to him.

I packed up my gear by the last bit of sunlight and was ready to leave by dark, but I had to wait a bit for the moon to rise so as to find my way out.

That Indian didn't make a sound. I figured that the icy water and those ropes must be pure torture but he didn't whimper.

When the moon came up full I had my riding horse out, the packhorse following with a lead rope from the saddle. Not fifteen minutes away I stopped.

Something black was working inside me. I couldn't keep my mind away from my dead family and what was worse I was getting closer and closer to the day I buried them. I knew I should have carved that Apache up some, but I couldn't stay around long or they'd get me and then they'd do to me just what they did to . . .

I jumped up and ran back up the trail. I ran hard and kept that black thought out of my mind. When I got near I pulled my knife. He didn't hear me come what with his own hurt and the sound of water. He was as alone as a man can be. Not even his tortured body could keep the black fear from screaming inside his brain. He was alone and frightened. He whimpered.

When he saw me, knife in hand, his eyes brightened and he almost smiled. He wasn't alone and someone would see him die. He began a chant, his death song, I guess. I cut the ropes. He couldn't move so I hauled him up on the bank and started a fire. He was still waiting for the knife. I put it back in its sheath and, with my hands, I made the signs that told him his life was his. He didn't believe me and when I left the fire I heard dry grass whisper as he staggered off to hide in the bush.

Two days later I was in Tombstone, a drink in my hand, standing behind Gene, watching him deal five-card stud. But my mind was on that Indian so I didn't hear Gene call me. Suddenly I knew that the whole loud saloon was quiet. I shook my head and then I realised that I was behind Gene in the spotter's hole. That's where a crooked gambler spots a man to signal the big bettor's hand. Gene was the big bettor in any game.

'You looking for an early grave, sonny boy.'

Men moved away from me and the players slid their chairs back away from the table, but they all kept their hands up above the table level or on it. The man opposite me put his hands up by his ears. He was white.

'You talking to me, mister?' I knew who he meant, but I couldn't think of anything else to say.

'Yes, boy. Get out of this place. Now!'

I didn't move, so he said, 'Get out of this casino and get out of Tombstone. I'll give you one-half an hour.'

Gene's eyes were cold as snake's. Blue snake eyes. I was standing, ready to draw. Gene was in his chair, shuffling cards. I knew I could get a shot off before he could, but he didn't seem to care, and a man looking at those go-to-hell blue eyes might just shoot a hole in the floor, or through the roof, while go-to-hell Gene put his shot right around your belt buckle.

Somehow the Indian's whimpering got to working at me again and I figured that if I was going to be alone, then I might whimper too, but I'd be damned if I would when there was anybody watching me.

'Well?' Gene's hands kept worrying those cards.

'As long as I got thirty minutes, I guess I'll have another drink,' I said. 'A man can get thirsty up in the hills.'

I walked over to the bar. Everybody moved out of my way. Behind me I heard Gene cackling. The bar noises came back. The drinkers were lined up two and three deep at the bar. Except that where I stood there was plenty of room.

There was a big clock at one end of the bar. Everyone there took turns looking at it and whispering. 'He's got twenty minutes more.' 'I say fifteen,' or 'Bet he runs out before she says twenty after.'

Those thirty minutes went by so fast that I had time for only three drinks. My throat was dry, even after the whiskey, so I ordered a beer. The bar cleared its length and I knew my time was up.

'Clem,' Gene said, 'give the boy a beer on my account.'

'Clem,' I said, 'better make it a short one.'

Gene laughed. Not a mean laugh but a happy one.

'Go on, scoot out, sonny, and don't bother grownups again.'

I drank the beer, all of it, without stopping. 'Mister,' I said, 'two nights ago I killed one Apache and turned another loose up in the Chiricahuas. For seven years I been taking care of myself. I am twenty-one years old, I have shot my Colt more than once. I am not going to be run out of Tombstone. Nor this bar, unless it happens to belong to you.'

'It does, boy, it does,' Gene said flatly.

'This bar is yours?' I asked.

'No,' Gene said. 'Tombstone is mine.' He laughed. 'Tombstone, boy, Tombstone!'

I backed up a bit and dropped my right hand to my belt buckle. Gene was leaning relaxed against the bar. I figured with that kind of advantage I could have taken him. I was wrong then, but I didn't find out until much later and by then I was just as fast as Gene, maybe a bit faster, although by then it would have been suicide for both of us in an even shoot-out.

'Clem,' Gene called, 'another quick beer for my young friend by the name of . . . '

'Bliss,' I said, worrying at the cork on the saloon's home-made beer. I got the cork in my teeth and it came out clean. So did Gene's gun. It was pointed right at that cork.

'You should be more *aguzado*, boy,' Gene said.

Along the border everyone speaks both Spanish and English some, and throws in words that seem to fit. *Aguzado* meant that I should have been ready. On my toes.

Anyway, someone in the back yelled, 'Shoot that *corcho* right out of his mouth, Gene. Ten bucks you can't knock the *corcho* out and not get blood on his lips.'

Gene slipped his .44 back in its quick-draw holster, put one arm around me and said, 'Clem, a drink for my friend, Corcho Bliss, noted Indian fighter, card kibitzer and raconteur. Drinks for the house.'

Clem looked down at his hands, pressed flat on the bar, and then up at Gene. Gene nodded 'Yes' so Clem grinned and began pouring drinks.

I got drunk that night. For the first time in my life. So drunk that when I woke up I was lying dressed, crossways in bed, in Missus Gorey's ten-dollar whorehouse. Gene was up already, shaving. That was when I threw in with Gene. He was ten years older and he taught me a few things about guns and cards and some about people before those bastards that ran the state decided we were not businessmen but bandits and set their dogs on us.

Gene went north and I moved on to El Paso. That had been twenty years ago. Twenty years of prospecting, gambling, hired gun, actor, and finally, that last shoot-out in El Paso. Twenty years and I was getting tired. I wondered what that man who said he knew Gene meant when he said we could have a million dollars. We! Even if it was fifty thousand it would be more than enough. I let my mind wander off and there I was, stocking my ranch when suddenly I got into an argument with myself as to whether I should run whitefaces on the well-watered part and longhorns on the rest or forget about the dry grass and concentrate on the watered part. Then I had to laugh. Corcho Bliss, forty-one years old and you start believing in a crazy gunfighter's 'lost treasure'.

'Hah,' I said out loud, 'I'll bet he's even got a map.'

The sharp bittersweet smoke from the charcoal fires hung over the valley that General Lara had picked for his camp. Men lazed around the fires sipping sweet *café de olla* and folding, not rolling, cornhusk and tobacco into cigarettes. Women scurried carrying wood or water. The sun was high now.

Although their rifles were out of sight every man had at least one short gun and a knife on his belt. Except for the women working, it reminded me of one of the old gold camps before the law moved in.

I reined my *grulla* up alongside Willy and Pearl. We just sat there, the three of us, watching. A matchstick of a man darted from behind a peeled-pole lean-to and hissed at us. A Mexican might not hear a bugle call but a hiss stops him in his tracks. He took about fifty short quick steps to get over to us although he couldn't have been more than fifteen feet away when he started. He had on dirty white shoes, pants, shirt and one of those jungle hats that Englishmen wear in the tropics. He didn't look English at all. He looked more like a Yaqui Indian who had got himself a scholarship to the Yuma State Prison and then had been thrown out because he was a bad influence on the rest of the students. His eyes were muddy shoe buttons with no light in them. He had a nose that must have been hit with a gun butt at one time and a scar ran down from one eye to his lips. It was the only pleasant thing about him. First impressions are often wrong and I found out later that Pablo Morales was not really as he appeared. He was a whole lot worse.

'Get off the horses by a goddamn now,' he said. His voice fit right in. It was flat, mean and, like his clothes, kind of dirty.

I swung off my horse, leaving the reins over the saddle horn, and the buckskin trotted off towards where I figured the creek must be. I started after him, thinking more of a cool drink of water for me than any worry about the horse foundering after our dry ride.

'No. You come, gringo, goddamn now! Boys watch the horse, goddamn!'

'Yes, goddamn right.' I wanted him to know that I spoke English too.

'Floyd, my boy,' Willy said, 'do not antagonise the gentleman. Let us see that great and noble revolutionary and, I might add, my dear and esteemed friend, General Lara.' At this point Willy looked sideways at the skinny man with the mushroom hat. 'Yes, let us visit with the general for a few minutes before we attend to our toilettes.'

Willy offered his daughter his arm and they strolled along, ignoring the dogs barking, an occasional scream of anger and one near machete duel. They might have been on their way to church. Pablo and I went on ahead. I walked and he trotted, leading the way.

General Lara was sprawled on a blanket in the shade of an open-sided lean-to. He had a bottle of tequila and one plate with coarse salt on it and one with a handful of quartered limes. Lara waved us down to the blanket. Pearl glared at him. Lara blinked at her. He couldn't figure her out any better than I could. Willy knew. He had been around all kinds of women and I guess he must have spent some time studying his daughter. He whipped out a handkerchief and spread it on a corner of Lara's blanket and helped her lower herself to a seat. I hunkered down on my heels and held out my hand for the bottle. Lara handed it to me. I bit into a lime and took a big swallow of tequila to wash the juice down. I had already wet a thumb and wiped it with salt. I stuck this up under my tongue. It helps your taster remember that tequila has a flavor.

'Yes, General. I do believe that the dust has dried my throat.' Willy tugged at the bottle until I let go and then swallowed three times without taking the bottle away to breathe.

When Lara got the bottle back he checked the level, turned his mouth down and then lifted the bottle up to finish it off.

'*Pablo, tráeme otra botella,*' Lara growled, and Pablo left in that slow sprint of his.

'And bring some more limes,' I yelled after him.

Across from me Pearl sat up straight, her hands twined, mouth open. She was looking right behind me and I knew why when I felt cold metal touch my neck. I sat very still.

'That's one of the new Colts,' Willy said. 'I congratulate you. A handy weapon if you keep the sand out of the action and remember to keep it on half cock. However, that is a bit careless.' Willy chatted to Lara as if he were discussing a young boy who had his pants on backside to. 'Your man has that pistol on full cock and the safety is off. Why he could kill my bodyguard and then I couldn't get to my delivery point and sell you my new machine guns.'

'Machine guns!' Lara sat up. 'Pablo, I told you to get me some tequila.'

The muzzle left my neck. I counted five and said, 'And don't forget the limes.'

'You don't give a *chingada* do you?' Lara asked.

'I sure do. But if he's going to kill me tomorrow, he might just as well do it today.'

Lara roared. It was an old revolutionary and bandit slogan twisted a little for the occasion. He took out his left-handed Colt and gave it to me. 'Pablo will kill you, but you should have a gun in your hand when he does.' He turned to Willy. 'Where are the machine guns?'

'In El Paso. They cost two thousand dollars apiece.'

'Two thousand dollars! Hah!' Lara snorted.

'That's what they *cost*, General. I sell them for three thousand dollars. I must make a profit.'

'And they call me a bandit.' Lara sighed. 'I'll take all you got.'

'It is a pleasure to do business with a man that knows his own mind. I can place them at any point across the river that you select, provided that it is not too far from El Paso.'

'You know the old Terraza Northern Ranch?'

'Yes,' Willy said, 'the little one north of the big one.'

'Right,' Lara said, 'the little one.' The little one was over a half a million acres. 'He's got a small house right on the river, maybe three *leguas* from El Paso. To the south.'

'Good,' Willy said. 'I have twelve Browning machine guns. That will be forty thousand dollars.'

He even stopped me for a minute. I'm not top-notch with figures, but I can multiply three by twelve. So could Lara. He got a black look and his voice turned flat. 'You mean thirty-six thousand dollars, my friend.'

'No,' Willy said sadly. 'I have transportation costs and I have hidden expenses with the border guard. Now, if you want to pick them up in El Paso, why then the original price stands.'

Lara thought about that for a minute, then nodded. 'Okay. I'll pay the extra costs. What else you got?'

Willy got out a pencil and, so help me, a block of orders. He must have had them clipped to his money belt. Willy proceeded to sell General Lara over a hundred thousand dollars' worth of arms. While he was closing the deal I saw Pablo approaching and nodded pleasantly to him. I kept my hand on the butt of the Colt. Pablo had his pistol in a cross-draw holster. It is a good rig when you're sitting but only just fair when standing. A lot of gamblers favor it. I eased to my feet. Pablo eyed me a bit and without looking at Lara asked, 'I kill this *pinche* gringo. No?'

'No,' Lara said. 'Not until after we get the guns. Then you shoot him. Or maybe he shoot you.' Lara laughed. 'Then we'll have a gringo *coronel* in our army, eh, gringo. What are you called?'

I took a deep breath. The time had come to use my

reputation. 'Corcho Bliss,' I said, smiling slightly, waiting for recognition.

'That's a funny name,' Lara said.

'All gringo names are funny,' Pablo replied.

'I thought your name was Floyd,' Pearl said.

'Just call me Gringo,' I said. I sat down again and Lara passed me the tequila.

Willy said, '*Sic transit gloria.*'

You can tell how cold it is by how many times a minute a cricket chirps. If you have a watch. Mine had been shaken loose when they stopped the train and I hadn't been able to find the new owner so I couldn't set the chirps to time. I rolled over on the straw *petate* and tried to wrap the ragged old serape around me another time but it couldn't be done.

Up north the Dipper was tipped clear over, its handle touching the Rio Bravo someplace north and east. It was near dawn. I shook my head and the crickets stopped. Either it was too cold for them too or they were in my head. I propped up on an elbow and saw a spark and then a bit of flame down the slope alongside the creek. It was all I needed to get me up and moving. Except for my legs. I rubbed and pounded them, but when I could get up, I did it like an old cow, hind legs first, then the front. The wind was icy and if there had been any wet in the sky it would have snowed. Those mountains can be cold in December.

The woman, no shape or age to her under a long *rebozo* and a sweater or two, was measuring coffee into a clay *olla* when I eased down on my haunches by the fire. My knee joints cracked just like the knotty pine in the fire, but she noticed the difference.

'You are getting old to be sleeping on the ground.' Her voice was deep and had a tequila edge to it.

'That's right. I have tried and tried to stop, but you get the habit and it's hard to quit.'

'I quit. I found myself a regular bed. It folds up. Two could sleep on it.'

With my hands on the cold ground, I swung around, like a monkey. My chest and the front of my legs were still cold, but thawed. The fire warmed my back, neck to toe.

'Sure,' I said, 'if the kids don't crowd.'

'No kids,' she said.

'How about a cup of coffee? I'm warm outside but inside I'm pure ice.'

'*Sí, joven.*'

I like that. Real Mexican. You're a *joven*, a young man, until you die unless someone is mad at you. Then the best you can hope for is to be an old bastard whose mother, if you had one, had met your father briefly and didn't even remember his name.

She dipped a good glazed-clay cup into the coffee. Her hand was brown, work-coarsened. The coffee was sweet with sugar. It burned my throat but it cut through the ice.

Light was just showing in the east. Now other small flames flickered throughout the camp. Soon there was the soft sound of palms slapping as the women patted out tortillas. The sound and the smell of wood smoke is as Mexican as *chile*.

She pulled out a handful of dough – wheat dough, not the corn dough of the capital – and began the rhythmic beat that somehow produced a thin, round tortilla, ready for the grill. Soon she had a half dozen cooking on an old piece of tin.

'You got a woman?' She was plain-spoken.

'No. Not exactly.'

'You got one, not exactly?'

Well, she had me there and I had to say 'No.'

'You want one?'

She had a tortilla in one hand and a ladle in the other. She was stirring beans. I was God-awful hungry. Her *rebozo* fell away and I guess she was a little prettier than Willy, but not much.

'I guess not.' I reached for the tortilla, but she snatched it back, sprinkled some *chile* in it, and, rolling it up like a cigarette, one-handed, she began to eat. The smell of beans, black and pungent with *epazote*, rolled over me. I remembered that I had gone almost two days with no more than some bits of lemon to suck on while I drank Lara's tequila. I was hungry.

'You wouldn't want to sell me a tortilla and some beans?' I asked.

'Why not. One *tostón.* Fifty centavos.' She held her hand out. The sun was up now. I moved away from the fire. I stuck my hands in my pockets. They were as empty as a hangover's canteen.

'Somebody's keeping my money for me,' I said. 'Just as soon as I find –'

There wasn't much point in my talking. She lost interest when I got as far as no money. It was almost warm now. I unwound that mangy *sarape* from me.

'I'll give you this gen-u-ine Navajo blanket for a bowl of beans and a tortilla or twenty.'

'Hah!' She didn't even turn around.

That did it. I ain't much on beating women, but that is not to say I won't rap one when the need is there. I drew back my right for a short rabbit punch and found about one hundred pounds of soft brown girl hanging on.

'Come and eat with me,' she said.

She was dressed warm, but there was no way of disguising the body. She was just as well built as Pearl and a whole lot easier to talk to. I put my arm around her and she smiled up at me with those great soft brown eyes and led me right over to that dark-skinned, blond-haired Texan's fire.

'Here he is,' the girl said.

'Have some beans,' he said.

I have always liked black beans with a touch of *epazote.* The clay dish he gave me held about a pint and I ate them before the girl could spoon some *chile* on a tortilla, roll it and hand it to me.

'You ought to force yourself to eat now and then,' the Texan said.

'I been hungrier,' I said.

'When?'

'About five minutes ago.'

He ladled me out another pint of beans. I ate those and a half dozen more tortillas. Then she gave me a cup of sweet coffee.

'Pass me a cigarette, Tex,' I said.

He looked startled, then grinned. 'Tex will do.' He handed me a pack of Bull Durham and I rolled me a smoke.

The girl took her food off away.

'How much did your friend stick Lara for?'

'About one hundred thousand in gold. You think Lara will come through?'

'He'll come through. Maybe he'll let the drummer across the lines to okay the gun shipment, but he'll keep the girl.'

Suddenly I didn't like the idea of old Lara being responsible for Pearl. 'He can't do that. Willy won't sell him any guns.'

'He don't much like his daughter?'

I got the point.

The sun was up full and I rolled my old *sarape* up and sat on it. Then I took my coat off. The girl hung her *rebozo* on a bush, and without that covering her shoulders and breasts, she looked even better.

Tex caught me looking at her. 'That one's mine,' he said.

'Shore. You did yourself proud, Tex. She got a sister around what's temporarily demanned?'

'No.'

He didn't add to it, so I kept quiet, but she was as bold as brass. When she took the coffeepot off the fire, she went all the way around so as to bend over and show me more shapely brown flesh than a celibate man ought to see.

'Get out of here,' Tex snapped at her.

She took her time and then, instead of leaving, she got the sun in between her skirts and my eyes and that didn't help either. I guess she didn't know what drawers were for anyway.

After she got Tex madder and me horny, she flounced off down the trail.

'None of my business,' I said, 'but you ever clout her one?'

'No,' he said. I don't know if he meant no, not just once,

or no, never, but I didn't get to ask him which because just then he got that wild look and started off again on the treasure.

'With a few packhorses we can take a million out, a million, Corcho!'

'Sure,' I said. 'I'll bet you even got a map.'

'I do! A rough one, but I don't need one. I got myself a fine guide.'

'Who?'

'Lara.'

'But you're talking about his gold, no?'

'Yep. And Lara's going to lead us up there. You and me.'

I shook my head slowly. I meant no with a big N. I wasn't about to follow Lara anywhere.

'He'll go. He has to. To get the gold for the guns.'

'You just said Lara'd keep a hostage. Why pay for the guns?'

'So he can get more. He'll try your side-kick out and if he delivers, Lara will deal with him.'

'Willy,' I said.

'Willy?'

'Yeah. My side-kick.' I laughed. 'He's my boss. The girl, Pearl, she's his daughter.'

'She'll be Señora Lara the nineteenth before long.'

I figured I had better have a talk with Willy. 'See you later.'

He jumped to his feet, his pale eyes crazy. 'Listen. We two can make more on this one haul than the Deacon ever got in his whole life. Ever.'

'You been smoking *mota* this early?' I pushed past him but he grabbed me. I never could stand anybody hanging on to me.

'Get them claws off me, you shit kicker, or – ' I left it there.

He stepped back, killing mad. Finally he sat down. 'Stay there a minute.' He drew circles in the dirt. He wouldn't look at me. He was that mad. 'Lara keeps a cave full of whatever money or valuables he takes from the wealthy ranchers and the cities. He must have between a half and a million dollars just in jewelry. You've been in those old haciendas . . . look' – he held out a hand – 'Lara's plundered over a hundred. You know what even a small hacienda is?'

'Yeah,' I said. 'A hundred thousand acres or so.'

'Real small. To organise a hacienda, you start out with a parcel of land. That's what one man can plow in a day with a yoke of oxen. Then you send a man on a horse to see how many parcels he can oversee in a day. That's a rancho. You put another man on a horse to see how many ranchos he can keep track of and you got a small hacienda. You add more riders and you got more ranchos. I've seen them with a private railroad just to travel across the hacienda.'

He knew his haciendas all right and I said so, but I didn't read his sign, not even a little bit.

'They were millionaires. They lived in France half the year. I know. I worked on more than one hacienda. Those women bought diamonds like we might buy silver *conchos* for our chaps. Diamonds, rubies, pearls, gold. We'll take whatever we can on a couple of packhorses and cut out.'

His voice was a little loud.

'Hold on, hoss. You really believe in that lost-treasure swindle.'

'It ain't lost. Lara knows where it is and so does Pablo Morales. And I heard enough to maybe find it. But I need you.'

'*La torre,*' I said. 'The tower. That's what the general said just before Lara shot away his voice box.'

Now Tex looked startled. 'The tower. That's it. They always ride out south, but the tower's north.'

'North where?'

'There.' He pointed north and a bit east. A big jagged peak some thirty miles away looked as if some old Indian god had tried to cork a volcano and only half succeeded. 'That's it. They leave south. We ride north, hide out where we can see the base, then track in.'

'Yeah,' I said, 'and meet them coming out.'

'You may not have to wait that long,' Tex said. He smiled and touched his hat. '*Buenos días*, my general. And you,

Coronel Morales.' His smile got sick so I turned, keeping my hands high.

It was Lara all right. Pablo had his Colt on full cock. I knew better than to ask if the safety was on.

'I shoot them both, General?' Pablo asked.

When Lara nodded, I decided to shoot Pablo. Not many people know this, but if a really fast man with a gun decides to draw and shoot, mostly he can get a shot off before a man, a good man like Pablo, can get the message to shoot from his brain all the way down to his trigger finger.

'One last thing,' I said.

General Lara held up his hand. We all froze just where we were. My mind was now on just one thing. Pablo's belt buckle. I heard Lara say, 'What is it, gringo?'

I drew and shot. Pablo was knocked off to one side and his finger jerked as my bullet hit him. It was a chance I had to take. It hit Tex chest high. He dropped like a sack of feed and I knew he was done.

'*¡Hijo de la gran puta!*' Lara whispered. 'Pablo had a gun on you and you with your gun holstered, My gringo friend, you are one great shooter.'

Willy appeared from nowhere.

'Corcho, why didn't you stop that man from shooting our friend Pablo?'

Our friend! That Willy. He pulled Tex's gun out of its holster and traded. He tossed my gun, the one Lara had given me to even things up with Pablo, in front of Tex.

'Yes,' Willy said. 'Corcho tried to stop that man, but Pablo was faster. They killed each other. Correct, General Lara?'

'Pablo was the best I ever had. He won battles for me. He was good at keeping men from deserting.'

'I'll bet he was,' I said.

'No,' Lara said. 'I'll have him shot.' He jerked a thumb at me.

'We go together, General,' I said. I meant it and Lara knew it. Red surged up that bull neck and turned his muddy skin the color of a flooded dry wash in the red-dirt country.

'And the guns,' Willy said. 'I'll need my bodyguard to get the guns.'

Lara stared at me for a while. That gun felt as if the cannon were a licorice stick and might just bend over if I pulled the trigger.

Pablo sat up just then and said, 'Are we winning, *mi general*? Where's my gun?'

Willy dropped to his knees and ripped open Pablo's shirt. There was a furrow from his middle to his ribs. I had shot pretty well. My bullet splatted against his big silver buckle, knocked his wind out and then plowed across his belly and nicked a rib before it dropped to the ground. I picked it up later.

'You should use a silver bullet if you ever take a shot at him again,' Willy said. He muttered something about were-wolves and vampires.

'He's all right,' Lara said. He grinned. 'That *Tejano* couldn't kill old Pablo.'

'I'm not a Texan,' I said.

'I know that, gringo,' Lara said. 'I'm talking about that *pistolero* that shot Pablo.'

'Yes,' Willy said. 'All's well that ends well.'

Lara yelped commands and some women carried Pablo off. I slipped the Colt back in my holster. Tex's girl gave Lara a cup of coffee. He pinched her bottom and she giggled. She had to step over Tex to get the coffee.

I didn't know him well but he was a man who lived chancily, as the Deacon used to say, and he deserved better. I picked him up and carried him up to the first pine. A young boy brought a shovel.

While I dug a grave for a barely known friend whose luck just plain ran out, Willy and Lara came to terms.

'You send a man with the money in gold to the bank in El Paso. I will be at the border with the guns. When the money is in the bank, they wire me at the Nopalito train station. Then I deliver the guns.'

'No,' Lara said.

'But General Lara, be reasonable. We must be businesslike.'

'When you got the money, why you want to give me the guns, eh?'

I though it was a pretty reasonable observation, but Willy was indignant.

'You don't trust me!'

'Sure, I do,' Lara said. 'But not with one hundred thousand dollars in gold.'

'How about a hostage?' I said. 'Then when the guns are in your hands, I just ride on over and join Willy.'

'Very good,' Lara said. 'That is what we will do. When I get the guns, just as you told me, the blonde daughter will be released.'

'That's not what I said.'

'No,' Willy spluttered. 'I will not leave Pearl as a hostage.'

'Then we shoot you all . . . well, maybe not the girl. Maybe I'll marry her. I have not been married for a couple of months,' Lara mused.

'However,' Willy added, 'let's not jump to conclusions. I will wire my bank a coded message. As soon as they receive the money, they will send the guns to the border and, upon seeing Pearl there, will make delivery.'

'No,' Lara said. 'I'll pay when I see the guns.'

'It's not businesslike,' Willy said.

'Who cares?' Lara said.

Those who cared didn't speak up. Willy wrote a message and one of Lara's captains, he had boots on, rode off to the nearest telegraph station. The guns were to be delivered to Lara. Willy didn't say anything about payment.

'And if Señor Corcho Bliss will take off his gun, I will feel better. I do not like a man close to me who can draw and shoot before I can pull a trigger.' Lara held his hand out.

I had filled up the grave and was lugging a couple of rocks to mark it. It seems to me that a man should have something left to show that he lived. Tex had no kids and Carmencita couldn't care less. So I wanted to mark a grave for him, even if there wouldn't be anything to show for it once the rains started.

'General Lara,' Willy said, 'do you promise to treat us well, do us no harm, and fulfill your obligations as to the payment for the guns? I ask you to give me your sacred word as an officer and a gentleman. Do you give me your word?'

'*Por supuesto,*' Lara said. 'I, General Lara, will not harm you in any way and the gold is practically on its way. After all, I want guns and more guns.'

'Good.' Willy beamed. 'Corcho, give the general your Colt new-model revolver.'

I didn't much like to, but there wasn't another game in town. I handed him the revolver, butt first.

'When will we go?' Willy asked.

'We is a lot of people,' Lara said.

It hit Willy a lot harder than me. I had never believed Lara and it always seems strange to me that the bigger liar a man is the quicker he is to be indignant about another.

'That man is infamous. A teller of lies. An unbridled rascal.' Willy looked at me, his damp blue eyes plaintive. 'He promised.'

I nodded. Lara had promised. And he kept his promise for at least five minutes. He might not have kept it that long except that he couldn't find an officer right away.

One of our guards told us that Lara was going to trade the blonde gringa for a trainload of guns that once you turned them on just kept shooting. I told Willy that someone should warn Lara about turning Pearl on, but he just told me to shut up. He seemed upset when we heard riders move out and someone said, 'Look at that gringa.' We couldn't see them. We were hog-tied and lying face to face inside one of those corncribs that a kid might have made with big matches. The corncrib was steaming hot when they left us there, but it was icy now. It must have been close to midnight.

'But Lara promised.' Willy sounded as if his daddy had promised him a new saddle and then delivered a manure fork.

'I guess he don't much care if we think too highly of him, Willy.'

'He will, sir. He will. I shall make him rue the day he lied to Willy Harper. Yes, I shall.'

'Willy,' I said gently, 'they are about to shoot us. Maybe in an hour or so.'

'No,' Willy said, 'you are absolutely and irrevocably wrong.'

They hauled us to our feet a few minutes later and I had to admit I was wrong about the time. I always thought they waited until sunrise, but then I guess they wanted to sleep in and nobody wanted to bother with us.

A lieutenant had our feet cut free but left our hands tied. I had got so I could tell the officers. The *coroneles* wore boots, the captains either boots or high-heeled riding shoes and the lieutenants regular work shoes. The lower ranks fastened their spurs to their huaraches or even bare feet, which were tougher than most boots, and I had even seen one old boy shining his feet before he rode off into town. Our lieutenant had just graduated, for he had his shoes in one hand and a Colt in the other.

Willy's mouth tightened up just like it was a Bull Durham sack and some cowboy had pulled the string. He stepped right out, straight as a ninepin, then he stopped. His tone was respectful, but commanding. '*Le suplico que me conceda el favor de permitirme orinar antes de pasarme por las armas. No es apropriado para un hombre morirse con sus calzones mojados.*'

Willy could really get at a Mexican. Who would refuse a man a last pee – specially when he wanted to die dignified and dry.

'*Si señor*. Where would you like to make water?'

'In El Paso,' I said, 'I need to pee too.' Nobody got the joke. Willy gave me a dirty look.

The scuffy-shoed lieutenant couldn't take his eyes off my calfskin boots. Without looking up he said, 'I think the wall of the house will do.'

My throat was as dry as it ever has been. I don't guess I had ever been scared before. Not like that. They had given us too much time to think.

Willy was fumbling away with his pants and I figured his fingers were that scared that they couldn't unbutton his fly when he suddenly whipped out a grenade, pulled the pin, and held the little piston down with his thumb.

'Don't move,' Willy said, 'or I'll blow us all up.'

'But you would die too,' the lieutenant said petulantly.

'So he should live ten seconds longer,' I said. 'You fool, we're dead anyway. You want to die too?'

He thought about it for a minute then shook his head. I held out my hand and he dropped the Colt in it. The Colt in my hand was just like a jolt of good whiskey in my stomach. Warmth and courage.

'What now, Willy?' I said. I had become a believer in that little man's big brain.

'Get your captain's horse,' he ordered the lieutenant. 'And I believe Coronel Morales left his bay gelding here.'

'No!' The lieutenant was shocked. 'He would kill me.'

'That, my dear fellow, is future tense. You are dead, dead, dead if you don't. That is present tense.'

'I'll do it,' the lieutenant said.

'*¿Oye, teniente, vamos a matar a los cabrones o no?*'

The shout came from one of the sleepy soldiers waiting to shoot us. He was no more than thirty yards away but still hard to see in the pale moonlight.

'Keep them away,' I suggested, and cocked the Colt.

'Of course,' he said. 'Just a minute. This one wants to kiss his horse goodbye.'

The men hooted and hollered. I looked at the lieutenant with new respect. While they repeated the joke ten times, as simple people will, we ambled over to the horses.

'Bridles!' I said.

The lieutenant came up with them.

'There are three!' I said.

'*Si, señor*. I think I better go with you, no?'

'Yes,' I said.

We found our horses quickly. They were picketed, not hobbled.

'No saddles!' I said.

'No saddles,' the lieutenant agreed a bit unhappily.

'Hey, lieutenant. What goes?' the suspicious one yelled, walking over.

'We do,' Willy answered. 'I have a grenade that I'll stuff

right up old Pablo's horse's ass if you try to stop us.'

The voice changed from rough command to frightened indecision.

'No, the *coronel* would kill us all, a little bit at a time.'

'That's right,' the lieutenant added. 'And don't shoot at us. You might hit Don Pablo's horse or General Lara's mare. I, myself, am riding Captain Delgado's horse and you know how much of a *cabrón* he is.'

'Lieutenant,' the man pleaded, 'order me to do nothing, please.'

'Very well,' the lieutenant ordered, 'do nothing and then go and tell the captain that we three disappeared ourselves sometime last night.'

I saw that he had dropped his badge of rank, the old worn shoes.

'Lieutenant,' I said as we walked the horses out of the camp, 'I have an extra pair of boots in my luggage. If we ever get to Chihuahua, they are yours.'

'A pair of boots!' he said, his eyes shiny.

'Yeah,' I said. I thought, 'If we could really "disappear ourselves" right now, I'd give you mine, too.' Spanish is a great language. Willy said it's the reflexive verbs. Glasses break themselves. Watches don't want to run. And the three of us were going to try to 'disappear ourselves' from the best group of hell-for-leather riders I had seen since the Deacon's bunch broke up.

I rode bareback for all one summer once with a group of tame Utes up along the Green River on the Utah-Colorado border, but I was almost twenty years younger then and I guess my legs were tougher. Anyway, what with the horse and me sweating I began to gall. The sun came up fast and hit us head on. Lieutenant Romero seemed all right but Willy was groaning and cussing.

He still had that grenade. He couldn't throw it for it would be heard a mile away and his thumb must have been aching fierce.

We had reached the foothills and were easing the horses along rabbit trails. We all looked back every couple of minutes, but there was no dust rising and I figured we could make it to the railroad line and then it would be just a matter of who got to us first, the Chihuahua train or Lara.

'Willy,' I said, 'let me have that thing.'

'You won't explode it?'

'I promise I'll not make any noise.'

'Here,' Willy said. His thumb was white around the knuckle.

He released his thumb and I pushed the button back down. Then I said, 'Whoa, boy,' and slid off that sweating, bony animal.

'No!' Willy cried. But he was too late. I had spotted a big round rock next to a prairie-dog hole. I dropped the grenade in the hole and rolled the rock over the top and moved back. There was a sound like a bull farting; the rock lifted a couple of inches and settled back down over the hole.

Willy slid down off his horse.

'I would have thought of that in time,' Willy said. He was miserable and needed to grumble.

'What say we walk a while,' I suggested.

'Excellent idea, Corcho, my boy. Save the horses.'

Willy was galled too, but it was like him not to admit it.

Romero looked puzzled. I said, 'Save the horses,' and left it at that. His feet must have had an inch of callus for he walked over cockleburs and broken mesquite branches that could have stuck through another man's shoes.

The sun was about eleven o'clock high when Willy brought the subject up: Water.

Romero asked, 'You want it now?'

'Sure,' I said, 'a nice cool glass of water.'

'There are no glasses,' Romero said. He had a belt knife that was somewhere between a cutlass and a cavalry sword. He tied his horse to a clump of rabbit brush and frowned at some big barrel-like cactus. One struck his fancy. He peeled a bit of skin from it, rolled the skin up into a straw and then cut a big slash in the cactus and hollowed the bottom like a half a cantaloupe. He stuck the straw down in the hollow and motioned Willy over. 'Suck,' he said.

A pool of liquid, clear and cool-looking, was gathering in the half-rounded hollow. Willy sucked. Stopped. He said, 'Why it's sweet. Cool, too.' Then he began to sip away.

Romero had one ready for me and I went to work on it right away. Willy was right – it was cool and a bit sweet.

'Now,' I said when I had had enough, 'if we could just teach the horses how to use a straw.'

'Easy,' said Romero.

He cut off an arm from a cactus and skinned it of all the stickers and then sliced it up like you would a loaf of bread. He put a half a dozen slices in front of his big bay. The gelding ate the pulp as if it were candy. We watered the horses that way.

'I've heard of water so muddy that you have to chew it so's to swallow,' I said, 'but this one is new to me.'

'The *buras* and *berrendos* get most all of their water that way,' Romero said. The *bura* is the big mule deer and the *berrendo* is an antelope, which reminded me that I was hungry.

'You couldn't carve me a steak of that cactus, could you?' I asked Romero.

That did it. He actually laughed. 'No, but when we get to the railway, I'll catch us a few rabbits.'

I shrugged. I could show him a few things about snares and deadfalls and the like. I took my coat off and laid it across my big black's bony back and, using a rock for a step, I jumped on without moving the coat. Willy couldn't do it so he finally climbed on and then slid his coat under him until he was cushioned somewhat. Romero just vaulted up. I suspect he was a whole lot closer to one of the horse Indian tribes than to any Spanish granddaddy.

We hit a small rise a few hours later and I spotted the tracks shining in the sun. About that time Romero caught a thin trail of dust four, five miles back of us. We had been crossing from one rabbit trail to another so they would have to ride at a walk, a slow trot at least, to track us. I figured we had maybe a half an hour on them. The hill was a bit rocky and that would help. I took a quick sight on the rails. They were running almost due south so we'd walk north, about a mile from the tracks, until nightfall, then we'd cross and hide out close enough to hear the train coming.

'It's our only bet,' I said out loud.

'What?' Willy asked.

'Send the horses on. Then strike out north along the track. I'll come last and cover our tracks.'

Romero got it right away.

'Without horses!' Willy said. 'We could die out here without horses.'

'That's right. And we could die a whole lot quicker with them.'

Willy thought about that, then he slid off his horse and sighed. Romero and I pulled the bridles up over the horses' heads and slapped them on the rump, not too hard, just to get them moving. We didn't want any change of pace to show. Lara had some Yaqui trackers with him and they were better than most bloodhounds.

Willy and Romero struck out. I walked backward, a step a minute, cleaning the tracks away with a bit of rabbit brush and then sifting sand down over the brushed-out track.

We were maybe fifty yards away when they came riding up, the tracker in the lead, reading our sign from his horse. They stopped where we had, to look around, and then went on, following our horses. I could see their heads as they rode up and over the high ground. There were twelve of them all carrying rifles.

I kept right on wiping out tracks. Willy got testy with me.

'Come on, man. Let's go. They'll chase those horses for hours.'

'What do you think?' I asked Romero.

'No,' he said. 'As soon as they get down in the soft sand again they'll know they're trailing horses without riders.'

Willy arched his eyebrows.

'Weight,' I said. 'Those Yaqui trackers don't miss a thing.'

'Juan,' he said, 'that's the tracker. He's mostly Apache. And they'll be back and ride a ring around that rocky ground until they cut our sign.'

Willy's eyes clouded over, then brightened.

'Well, then,' he said, 'why not brush our tracks away right up to the railroad, then walk the rails away from here.'

That Willy. All he needed was a few details and he would come up with a plan. Both Romero and I nodded and I said, 'Willy, if you was just a bit prettier, I'd kiss you.'

When I backed up on to the railway, the rails were burning hot from the sun. Willy and Romero were waiting for me when I looked up.

'Go on,' I yelled. 'Keep on the rails for a mile or so and then duck off into the nearest cover.'

They took off and I sifted the last bit of sand over a boot track and tossed the bit of rabbit-brush broom to one side. I eased myself up on the rail and took two steps before I slipped off. My boot heel caught a tie and clipped a piece of wood off. I squatted and pulled off my boots before I rubbed dirt deep into the new wood.

The walking was easier without my boots but my feet were burning from the hot iron rails by the time I heard Romero call. He had picked a dry wash running under the track. They had run a culvert through and then packed rock around it, but on each side the wash was at least six feet deep and not quite that wide. The occasional heavy rains had left a slick surface so hard that I could walk over it without leaving a track. They were waiting for me just around a bend below a stunted mesquite that leaned over the wash enough to shade the south wall and a bit of the floor.

We sat with our back to the wall and our legs and feet out in the sun.

After a while I felt my skin go cold on me. I tapped Willy and put my hand to his mouth. Romero felt something, too. Then I saw shadows of two sombreros pushing out of the deep shadow on to the white sand floor of the gulch. Someone was standing with the sun to their back looking down into the gully. I eased my legs back and hugged my knees in tight. So did Willy and Romero. The hats got bigger until we could see the shadows' shoulders, too. Cactus and mesquite were high along the lip of the dry wash or they would have seen us. After a minute they moved away. The worst part was they hadn't said a word. We didn't either.

I drew a picture of a sun in the sand, then rubbed it out and showed a new moon. They both got the idea quick. I sealed my lips with a finger Indian sign-language style and there we sat, waiting for the sun to go down.

An Indian can sit for hours waiting for a rabbit to pop out of its nest or a deer to wander within bow shot. I asked a Ute once what he thought of while he waited. He said, 'Nothing.'

I could never do that or I'd take to cutting my initials in my new fancy boots. So I remember things I've done that were fun or just exciting. Like the time we got $50,000 in specie from the Union Pacific. We hit the train just before the railway trestles at the Green, where it's wide and muddy just inside Utah from the Colorado line.

I was only twenty-three then. It was the Deacon's last job and I think he did it just to show he could. Still, the telegraph was too much medicine for us. We'd cut the lines, but they still got the word out quicker than we could ride.

We had two men with red lanterns at the bridge with no guns showing and four on the train. Then there was one man with the horses, two for each man along with a month's rations and the brand-new 1892 Winchester .30-30's that used smokeless powder.

I was on the train. We carried Colts in shoulder holsters and we had sawed-off Remington pump shotguns broken down in our suitcase. By the time the train began to brake we would assemble the pumps. The tubes held five cartridges and there was one in each chamber, all loaded with double-aught buckshot.

There were four cars. I was on the last one. The one next to the caboose. It was the smoker. This was big medicine, the smoker. All men, for one thing, and most of them had a gun someplace. There were maybe fifteen there but I remember only three. One was a mean-looking coyote of a man. The kind that would grin up to his ears, all the time sneaking out one of those women's .32 pearl-handled revolvers. Then there was a big roughneck who looked dumb enough to try to eat a pound of buckshot. And there was a well-dressed gambler sitting off by himself. Dark, but with those ghost eyes he could have been the Deacon's younger brother, about my age or younger. He was practicing a false cut. The only reason I knew he was practicing was the sound of his fingers and the cards blurred when he riffed the deck. So I knew when the cards slapped together what he was doing.

We had a few minutes so I sat down by him. There was a table between us.

'Play a little poker?' I asked.

'Sure thing. Limit?' He had a good grin, white against his dark face. You wanted to trust him. I guess that's why he was a sharp.

'Let's say showdown for a hundred dollars,' I said.

His eyebrows jiggled just a little bit.

'Your medicine.'

He dealt me a pair of deuces and himself a pair of jacks. When he passed the deck to me, I dealt and lost.

'Two hundred,' I said.

He just nodded. He dealt me jacks and took the pot with queens.

'Two dollars,' I said.

His eyebrows danced that time.

I dealt him four aces and took the pot with a straight flush. He knew what I was doing but he sure didn't know why.

'You won,' I said. 'Poker's your game.'

His right hand suddenly just had to play with his string tie. I was right sure he had a hideaway gun, same as me.

'Yes,' I said. 'You stick to poker. You play your game. And I' – I tapped him on the chest – 'I'll play mine. You stay out of my pots and I'll leave yours alone. Okay?'

He frowned, but he nodded yes.

'Remember that,' I said.

Then I saw the big cottonwoods on the Green. We had one minute. Then the train was braking hard and I had to brace my feet against the potbellied stove. By the time we came to a halt I had the pump together. Everybody was talking except the gambler. He looked at me, then put his hands deep in his pants pockets and began to whistle softly.

I fired a load out a window, glass and all. It was silent enough then.

'I got five more loads in here. All double aught. If you stay put, hands on your shoulders, nobody gets hurt. Hell,' I said, 'we don't want your gold, just the railroad's. Now take it easy and no shooting. Anyone here's a stockholder in Union Pacific, tell me and I'll give him his share.'

That did it. The big man laughed and sat down. He didn't put his hands up but I didn't push the issue. The coyote didn't either so I took a step and rapped him with the barrel. He walked sideways into the stove and lay there.

The big man glared. 'I ain't got my hands on my shoulders.'

'I know,' I said, 'but I trust *you*.'

He grinned and looked around, proud as he could be. 'That goes for everybody here,' I said. 'If your hands tire, hold on to the seat ahead. I don't want to hurt anyone, but I get nervous when I can't see a man's hands.'

'You the Deacon?' the big man asked.

'No. My name's Frank. Jesse's up front with the Younger brothers.'

When they got through laughing, I knew we were all right. Nobody will pull a gun when he's laughing unless he's half crazy.

Just then the train whistle blew a long and two shorts, 'D' in Morse code. 'D' for the Deacon. He liked when people knew about him although he pretended not to. He'd be as secret as a Ute Indian making medicine, then he'd pull a stunt like that.

'That's all, gentlemen.' I chucked the shotgun out the window and walked out on to the platform between the cars. I jumped down and stood still then to get my eyes used to the dark. Somebody rapped on the glass with a gun barrel and I jumped. When I came down I had a gun in my hand. I heard the gambler's voice.

'Friend. The little man just went out the other side. After the scatter-gun I'd say.'

'I owe you one,' I whispered.

'Tex!' I spoke out loud. 'The gambler!'

'What?'

'*¿Que?*'

I startled Willy and Romero. Me, too. Suddenly I was back in a dry wash in Mexico. I looked up. The sun was easing down into the cactus-covered flatland. It was time to go.

'Let's go,' I said.

'What was all that about Tex?' Willy asked.

'I just remembered a favor I owed Tex.' It wasn't much of a favor I returned Tex, but it was the only one I'd ever be able to do for him, now. Except maybe put another bullet an inch or so higher in Pablo Morales' belly. I never did like those fancy big silver buckles.

Up on a mesa a coyote yipped. Another answered and then there were a dozen singing at the moon. I didn't like that moon. It was bright. Bright enough to shoot birds by if they flew between you and the moon. But we had no choice. It was walk away to a grade and try to slip on the Chihuahua train as it slowed down. Of course it wouldn't be much of a grade in this country. We could wait until light and try to stop the train by waving our arms at it. This last plan was not seriously considered by anyone except Willy, who figured the train would not only stop but back up to El Paso so he could set about trading the guns for Pearl.

We had walked for about three hours and I was plenty tired of trying to take steps big enough for three ties or dancing along with cute little steps that hit every tie. The short steps suited Willy. Romero walked barefooted along the rail.

Romero knew about the train first. He felt it through his feet.

'Which way?' I asked.

'To Chihuahua.'

'Then we'll wait for another,' Willy said.

'Willy,' I said, 'there won't be another train for a week, maybe never. In Chihuahua we can buy enough horses to change off mounts, and if we ride nights and hole up days, we can be in El Paso in four days.'

'And Lara will be there in three,' Willy said.

'No he won't,' I said.

Then Willy heard the song coming out of the night, louder even than the steam engine. It was 'La Cucaracha'. Whenever Lara's men got drunk or bored, they sang about the cockroach, which was a Model T Ford that wouldn't run unless it had a few cartridges of marijuana to smoke.

'Lara's got himself a train,' Romero said. 'He's going to take Chihuahua.'

'Without my guns?' Willy seemed hurt.

'If he rides this train right into town, he won't need machine guns,' Romero said.

'He's right, Willy. If he's off for Chihuahua, he'll have Pearl with him on that train. And no matter what, he'll still want the machine guns. If he takes Chihuahua, he'll want them for the fighting in the South. If he doesn't, he'll need guns to keep the Federal troops off his neck.'

'All right,' Willy said.

'I'll try it, Willy,' I said. 'If I make it aboard that train, I'll come back with horses.'

'We'll all ride the train in,' Willy said.

'Sure, just buy tickets from your old buddy, the Napoleon of the West.'

'Why not?' Willy said.

Romero said, 'If they slow down, we could slip in one of those cars with the horses.'

'Rocks,' Willy said.

And rocks it was. Romero took one side and I the other. We built a pile of big rocks. One I rolled up on to the track was a young boulder. When the train got close enough that the light was sweeping the track a hundred yards away, we ran off to the side and down the track towards the caboose.

The brakeman braked. Officers shouted. Guns were cocked. I heard Lara yell, 'Push the *pinche* rocks off the *pinche* track.' The engineer slowed down to a walk, the cowcatcher sent the rocks down off the roadbed, and we darted out of the brush and slid into a horsecar. We hung on with the door open until the train was moving normally. The horses were already nervous from the train and when one snapped at me I rapped him across the nose with Romero's Colt. Romero began talking to them and they quieted some. We shut the door and waited.

Every once in a while Romero would look at Willy. When he didn't, I would. Willy finally got mad.

'Stop eying me, you third-rate stable hands. I'll think of something.'

It took a while, but when Willy came up with the plan, it was big medicine. When he talked it seemed like it would work. When he stopped it was too wild. Still, we decided on his plan, mainly because we couldn't come up with anything else. Not better, even. Just anything.

Willy's plan had one virtue. It was simple. We would saddle five of the better-looking horses, and when the train stopped, we would lead them out; there would be no time for a plank walkway, so Romero would stand by with an extra bridle and use the reins as a whip. We saddled the two extra horses in case one broke a leg or got away from the man hauling on its reins. Then at a dead run we would go on ahead and warn the Federal troops. They would counterattack, flank the train, capture Lara, his army, the train and Pearl.

Willy was worried about Pearl's virtue, which I pointed out was about the same as worrying about a female jaguar. Willy got mad.

'You have the sensibilities of a Digger Indian.'

'I knew some Snake Indians once,' I pointed out, 'and they was just as sensible as they could be. Why they didn't believe in hanging garlic around their necks nor drinking salty water to ward off rheumatism or – '

'Oh, shut up.' Willy was not in a good mood.

'Lara won't touch her,' Romero said, 'until they're married. He is a very moral man with women. He has never taken a woman without marrying her first.'

'Will he have a priest in his army?' Willy asked.

'No. My general hates priests. He shoots them on sight, except when he's ready to marry again.'

'When do you think he might find a priest?' Willy asked.

'There aren't many left,' Romero said. 'Maybe that's why he wants to take Chihuahua, to find a priest.'

It was still dark when the train stopped, although the sky was turning gray on the eastern rim. I was crouched, ready to drop out, when two men came running up out of the dark and slammed a couple of planks nailed together up against the door. It was a rough, but good, unloading ramp for the horses.

Romero and I waited, one on each side, for the door to slide open. I took the first man and yanked him inside. I tapped his temple with my gun barrel and held him until Romero got his man with a shovel handle. We dropped them out on each side of the ramp. It was almost light now. I led the first horse down and mounted. That was a mistake.

'Hey, what you doing on the general's new horse?'

'Let's go,' I yelled and rode off. I heard the other two horses clatter down the ramp after me and then we were away. It was not light enough to run the horses, but then it was too dark to shoot. Willy closed up alongside me and Romero pulled in behind him. There was a lot of yelling and shouting. I heard Lara's voice and then silence.

'They won't dare shoot,' Willy said. 'They don't want to warn the Federales.'

The first yip could have been Apache but it was Mexican and it came from no more than a pistol shot away. A trail broke through the brush away from the track and I spurred my mount on to it. The light came quick now. The trail broke out into a clearing and up ahead I could see the small outbuildings, adobe all of them, huddled around the main buildings of Chihuahua.

Behind us there were a few scattered shots, then a regular fusillade. Up ahead I could see uniformed men wheeling guns into place. I yelled as loud as I could and waved my hat.

'Don't shoot. No! No!'

Willy and Romero joined in. We lashed our horses into a dead run. It was plenty light now. Half Lara's cavalry was riding after us. They were all shooting and some of the bullets were whining by. Then the Federal troops opened up. The first bursts from the cannon hit just between us and Lara's troops. Then we were in rifle range and I could see the little bright spots as the infantry turned loose on us. I had never thought that so many men I had never seen or even thought of before could be that eager to kill me.

We were still yelling and waving our hats but no one seemed much interested in us except as targets. Off to our right a column of ragged soldiers was double-timing it, heading into us at an angle. They were shooting too, but toward the Federal troops.

'Let's ride through the lines,' I yelled. 'It's our only chance. Maybe if they see us in there, with our hands empty, we'll get a chance to talk.'

Willy nodded yes. He shook his head sideways after though to show me what he thought of our chances. Romero looked bored.

A shell burst almost in front of us. My horse shied, almost fell, and then we were all three in the lines. Men were running and dropping. I saw an officer, sword in hand, and I fairly jumped from the saddle, hands high.

'I'm an American,' I yelled. 'I was a prisoner of Lara.'

'Yes, sir,' he said. 'I ask that you give me and my men protection.'

He shoved his sword at me, hilt first, and I took it.

'What?' My jaw dropped.

'We are your prisoners, sir. Be humane.'

'Huh?'

Back of me the cavalry had lassoed the three cannon and drug them off to one side. There were a few shots, but mostly the Federal troops were standing still, their hands high. The ragged infantry troops were holding guns on them.

A general, I guessed, because of his blue, red and gold coat, rode up behind them. He was beaming.

Lara rode up, followed by Pablo Morales. I looked from one to the other, the sword still in my hand.

My captured officer said, 'That was the wildest charge I have ever seen. You are a brave man. And an excellent tactician. We expected a frontal attack by way of the railroad.'

'Oh, no!' I groaned. 'I had to lead the attack that took Chihuahua.'

Lara and the other general trotted up.

'You *cabrón*,' Lara said. 'I ordered you shot, you *cabrón*.'

'Sorry, General Lara,' I said. 'I never had proper military training.'

'I'll fix that, you *cabrón*,' Pablo said.

The general in the pretty coat didn't seem to hear the other two.

'My hero!' he said. He threw his arms around me and, hopping up and down so as to reach my face, he kissed me.

'Come on now. Stop that!' I pushed him away.

'General Lara,' the blue-and-red-and-gold general said, 'I wish to congratulate you. The President shall hear of your surprise attack. You are an excellent tactician and an even better judge of men. What is this man's name and rank, General?'

By his tone I was getting the idea. There are generals and generals. I guess Lara was maybe a Number Four one, but this old boy in the pretty coat was a Number One general.

Lara was thickheaded all right, but he wasn't a bit dumber than a ten-year-old sheep-killing coyote.

'General Castillo, this is Captain . . . uh, that is, Major Bliss, one of my great cavalry officers, the *cabrón*.'

'Major,' General Castillo said. 'Major . . . no. I think maybe not. What do you pay a major?'

'He gets third choice in *vino* and women and eats with me. Sometimes we split up some money, then he gets half of what Pablo gets.'

'He is now a *coronel.* Second choice with *vino* and women.' He grinned and looked at me. 'Half as much money as you, and as a special reward, you don't have to eat with General Lara.'

While General Lara was busy explaining to the Number One general how the great and unexpected cavalry charge had occurred to him and why he hadn't let him know about it, I saw Pablo trot over to where two soldiers were trying to shut up a woman, a *soldadera* by the crossed cartridge belts she wore.

Pablo couldn't stop her shrieks and I figured he might shoot her if the big general wasn't there. She got Lara's attention by yelling louder than he was talking.

'What's her trouble, Pablo?'

'She lost her husband today.'

'So did a lot of others.'

He turned away, but she broke loose and before Lara could move she had her arms around his legs.

'Let me alone, woman.' His voice would have sent anyone else running.

'I have three small children. Who will feed them now my husband is gone? What will I do? Help me, my general. I beg you.'

Lara twisted his collar. I whispered, 'Pay her a few months' salary to tide her over.'

'Here,' he said, 'here's a thousand pesos. Now go on and help the revolution. Maybe you'll find a man that lost his wife.'

'God will pay you. God will pay you.' She was smiling when she walked away, counting the silver pesos from Lara's leather bag into her own canvas *mochila.*

'General Lara, you are not only an inspired tactician but a humane, kindly man. I am going to write a memorandum to every staff officer in the army, and to our constitutional President to advise him of your compassion. Go with God, my General Lara.' The old gentleman general, tears in his eyes, strode off.

'I never heard him talk about another general like that,' Pablo said.

'Hah!' Lara was beaming.

'But,' Pablo said, 'her old man is downtown drinking tequila in a whorehouse. He gave her the slip right after the battle.'

'That no-good *cabrón*,' Lara said.

'I'll go get the money back,' Pablo said.

'No. Wait.' Lara rubbed his head and I could just hear the words of the top general echoing back and forth in Lara's big skull.

'But she owes us the money. Her old man is not dead!' Pablo said.

'Yes, he is,' Lara said. 'Find the *cabrón* and shoot him.'

Just give Lara a minute to think and he could solve about any problem that might come up.

'Now, General.' The Number One general waved at Lara. He pulled Lara away. 'Let's see to the city.' He looked back at me. His salute was as casual as a wave. 'I'll see you later.'

Pablo trotted off.

'Have fun,' I said. Pablo looked back. If he could have bitten me, I would have died before sundown.

'I'll see *you* later,' Lara said. He and a group of his personal bodyguards rode off. Some of them were already half drunk.

I sat down. So did the officer, hands still high. Willy came limping up. His face was black. His coat was half torn off. Romero followed behind him; he could have been looking for a cigarette butt.

'Where's Pearl?' Willy said.

'We'll go call on her just as soon as we get cleaned up.'

Romero was eying the officer. He asked to borrow my Colt. Except it was his. Anyway I told him no.

'Lara shoots the officers almost always,' Romero said.

'No. We're going to trade this one his life.'

'For what?' both Romero and the officer said.

'For his boots,' I said. 'See if they fit, Romero.'

His face fell apart then. His ears began to wiggle back to make room for that grin.

'Sure,' he said. 'Sure they'll fit.' They were tight, but they looked fine. It took a while for that grin to wear off. And before the boots stretched it didn't really matter anymore.

My prisoner, Captain Raul de la Vega, lately of the Federal Army, turned out to be a jewel. He led us to what he called his quarters. This was a house about the size of a small hotel.

While we shaved and washed, he painted a big sign to hang outside. It read 'Coronel C. Bliss, of the Triumphant Northern Army of General Lara's, Quarters.' You couldn't read the first part unless you stuck your face up next to the sign. But to make up for the little letters, he painted 'General Lara's, Quarters' in letters about three feet high. It would discourage foragers, he said.

His uniforms were too small in the shoulders for me and the legs were short, but I tucked them in my boots and left one of his shirts half buttoned. Willy said I looked rakish. I didn't care. My old shirt smelled worse than week-old pulque.

'We must see Pearl, now!' Willy said for the tenth time.

'Right, Willy,' I said. I put a flask of French brandy in my hip pocket and stuck a couple of Captain de la Vega's fine Cuban cigars in the waistband of my pants.

I was out the door when the captain caught me by the arm. 'One moment, my *coronel.* Your shoulder stars.' He pinned some silver stars, two it was, I think, on each shoulder. He had the sword in a scabbard and tried to buckle that on me too, but I wouldn't let him.

'No, Raul. I got a knife someplace that's just the right size to carry and I don't plan on fighting no duels with that overgrown Green River special.'

'It is from Toledo. It belonged to my grandfather.' Raul was hurt.

'I mean that a sword like that should stay in your family. Pass it on to your son.'

'As you wish.' He was still mad so I asked him to come along.

'I am your prisoner.' He clicked his heels, but he forgot he had no boots and he groaned when his bare heels cracked, one against the other.

'Come on,' I said. 'We'll get you a job in the other army. You fussy about who you work for?'

'No,' he said. 'Providing I do not have to fight. I do not like to fight.'

'Why?' Romero asked.

'I get frightened,' Raul answered.

Romero couldn't figure that out.

Willy was pushing and pulling at me so I went along out with him. Raul yelled something about boots, but there wasn't time. Willy said, for petty delays, so we trooped off, Raul in his bare feet, groaning at each step. So was Romero; he wasn't used to shoes, let alone tight parade-ground boots.

We made our way about three blocks down the street, pushing drunks out of the way and jumping for a doorway when a squad of drunken Laristas galloped by.

'Willy,' I asked, 'where are we going?'

'To get Pearl, of course.'

'Oh,' I said. 'And where is Pearl?'

'Why, she's . . . I would venture to say . . . ' Willy ran down. He sat down on a doorstep. His face lost its red, even from his nose, so I knew it was bad. 'I don't know, Corcho. I don't know.'

Romero spoke up. 'That blonde will be pretty close to General Lara now that the fighting's over.'

'Of course,' Willy said. He brightened up right away, but then he remembered. 'We don't know where Lara is.'

'Sure we do,' Romero said. 'Where's the biggest whore-house in town?'

'Gentlemen,' De la Vega said, 'follow me. I know all of the major cultural attractions of Chihuahua.' I laughed. He shrugged and led off.

'Let's go,' Willy said. His nose was bright red again.

Two of Pablo's killers were at the door. They knew me all right, but they didn't say anything except that we couldn't come in.

'Why?' I asked.

'The general don't want no more guests. The wedding is about to start and this old whorehouse is full. Not even a *cucaracha* could get in.'

'Do you want to go in, my *coronel*?' the captured captain asked. 'For if you do, I can get us in. It is easy if I apply my knowledge of the intricate niceties of the Mexican soldiers' mental processes. I shall apply scientific stimuli to known sensory receptors. It cannot fail.'

'Go ahead,' I said. 'Stimulise them.'

'Thank you,' he said. His eyes widened, his lips turned up slightly and his voice rang with sincerity. 'Out of the goodness of your hearts, my brave soldiers, let these men in. The lonely father, the lovesick swain. In the name of humanity – ' One soldier blew smoke at him. The other yawned. 'In the name of humanity,' he repeated, 'and ten dollars in gold, let them in!'

The doors swung open. We pushed in. The locks clicked shut behind us. The sweet alfalfa smell of marijuana, or *grifa*, as they called it, was thicker than tobacco. There were different layers of smell in that room. Willy dropped a handkerchief he was holding to his nose, and in bending down to pick it up, he almost stayed there. After a while I noticed him there, kind of like a bird dog on a point. I hauled him up.

'That smell,' Willy said when he could breathe again, 'weighs at least two hundred pounds to the square foot. Don't let it pile up on you. Whew!' He forgot about his handkerchief and began pushing the air down away from his nose.

I guess the smell was pretty heavy where Willy was. I was

up a foot or so higher and it wasn't so bad. Now and then a smell like a wet dog would hit me or I'd get a wave of perfume so strong that it would leave my face wet. I don't know which was worse.

The floor was covered with soldiers and girls. Some of them may not have been whores, but only because they lacked the natural ability. I was a head taller than anyone there, but as all the men wore two-foot-high hats, I didn't stand out none.

Willy pointed to a stairway. There were four soldiers there. One was an officer. He had a self-cocking Smith and Wesson revolver that he was yanking out of its holster, trigger-cocking it, then letting the hammer fall back short of exploding a round before he spun it back into its holster. After each performance he would grin and look around the room. I tugged at Willy and we pushed through the crowd over to the soldiers.

Just as we got there, the slim officer twirled the gun and shot himself. He tumbled down on the floor, his three guards around him. Willy and I walked by, up the stairs and around the corner right up to the eye-high muzzle of Pablo Morales' repeating pistol. 'Who you shoot, gringo?'

'Nobody. My gun's clean.'

'I demand an audience with General Lara,' Willy squeaked, higher than usual.

'He's trying to get married,' Pablo said.

'It will only take a minute,' Willy said. 'I have to find my daughter, Pearl.'

'Put your hands up higher,' Morales said. I did.

He grinned. 'She getting ready to get laid by the general.'

Willy's face went white. He started forward. Morales backed up a step. I never would have believed it.

'You dare speak of my daughter, you son of the great whore.' Willy could use a cuss word or two if he felt the need.

'Hold it, Willy,' I said. 'Let's get Lara out here where we can talk.'

'No,' Morales said.

'Then you better start shooting,' I said. 'And General Lara told you to let me alone. You going to shoot me?' I took a big breath and moved forward.

He went back one and yelled, 'One more step and I kill you by goddamn, you *cabrón* you.'

I took the step. His eyes blazed as yellow as those of a coyote in a trap. And not as friendly. But he didn't shoot. Instead he yelled, 'Get the general.'

The general was as happy as I had ever seen him. He even grinned at Willy and me. '*Hola, cabrones.* Where you been? We are going to have ourselves a real *baile.*'

'Happiness!' I said.

'Where's Pearl?' Willy asked.

'Who's Pearl?' De la Vega wanted to know.

Romero pulled a tablecloth off the nearest table. A bottle and glasses shattered on the floor. He shrugged and set about shining his boots. De la Vega pointed out a spot he had missed and Romero went back over to catch it. De la Vega's feet were not so blue as they had been; still, I meant to get him shod when I had the time.

'Where is my innocent daughter?' Willy demanded.

Just then there was a glass-shattering regular catfight. A young girl came headfirst down the stairs. I picked her up, but she was limp.

The general shook his head and downed another tequila. He waved a hand, at heaven I thought, but he said, 'First floor. Up there. Dressing for the wedding.'

Willy started up the stairs, but he only got halfway before a clay *olla* caught him flush on the forehead. He turned and slowly walked back down the stairs. He sat down and then keeled over. I sat the girl alongside him. The general looked at me. 'Do you think a good beating would do anything for that gringa?'

'No,' I said, starting up the stairs, 'but it will shore make me feel better.'

He thought that was funny, so I picked up a small table, and holding it in front of me, I went on up. There was a door at the end of the first landing. I kicked it open. She was ready to repel boarders, a lit kerosene lamp in her hand. I caught it on the table and yelled, 'Pearl!' She slung a brass candlestick holder at me. I caught it on the table, too. 'It's me – Corcho!'

The fighting lines eased off and her mouth turned up, then down. 'Oh,' she wailed, 'where's Willy? What'll I do, Corcho?' She ran right into my arms. I flinched and tried to cover up, but she only meant for me to hold her, which was pretty nice once I got over worrying about getting kneed.

'Willy is laid out on the bottom of the staircase. You got him a little off center so he shouldn't be out much longer.'

'That was Willy?' She turned on the tears. In between sobs I got the story. They told her we had ridden on ahead to check on some new guns that the other general, the Number One, had wanted and to see if Willy might be able to get some of the same kind for Lara. When they rode out of camp, she thought we would be waiting up ahead. Then they went on the train. Lara got her a separate compartment, so she felt that there wouldn't be any hanky-panky, but then he got too close to the two-way mirror and steamed it up on her side too. When she realised that the gold-leaf design was mostly holes, Pearl got mad and threw a chair through it. She beaned the general but not before he got an eyeful. She was strip naked when she let the chair go. He woke up talking about the gringa with the body. She hung a sheet over the broken window-mirror, dressed fast, and stayed away.

But Lara had seen that body and decided he had to marry it. Besides, he hadn't been married for several months. Social life is slow up in the mountains.

They have a little caterpillar-type crawler in Mexico they call *cara de niño* that's said to be poisonous. It has a kind of baby face, with the coldest blue eyes you might ever want to see. Pearl's eyes put me in mind of that little baby-faced worm. Still, I tried to tell her what I had in mind about switching girls.

'Pearl,' I whispered, sticking my face up close so that no

one else could hear. I patted her big, firm tail to comfort her.

That was a mistake. She cracked me one on the side of my head that brought tears to my eyes. I grabbed her hands.

'Pearl, I'm going to get another one of those girls here so's the two of you – ' I meant to say that they could switch places and somehow I could smuggle her out, but she cracked me one across the shins and, even with my boots to cushion the blow, it hurt. I got mad and threw her over on to the bed. She kind of bounced off the wall and slid down on to the bed. I went over to see if she was all right and jumped back just in time. She still had fight in her. So I said, 'If you want to marry Lara, just say so. If you don't, shut up and stay here.' I left without looking back.

It didn't take me long to find a girl about Pearl's build. Except her skin was honey-colored, as much as I could see, which was maybe about two-thirds of her. Her eyes were kind of green, but her hair was black. She could have been Pearl's first cousin on the Latin side. She was sitting on a big captain's lap. At least he had boots on so I couldn't been off more than a grade, either way. The way she was moving her plump little cheeks around on his lap I figured her price and his blood pressure were running neck and neck. His *compañeros* were sprawled asleep in their chairs. Outside of a few shots and yells and bottles crashing, it was quiet so I figured they wouldn't move for a day or so. The captain had her dress unbuttoned and pulled down over her shoulders, and if she had ever had a brassiere on, he must have chucked it over his shoulder.

She was talking to him about twenty pesos in silver, and when he mumbled something about ten, she stuck one of her golden-colored titties in his face and then wriggled around a little faster. He gave up and she jumped off his lap and led the way. I followed them. As soon as they made the turn, I stepped up behind him and hit him as hard as I could on the back of his thick neck. He went down and stayed. The girl turned then and got ready to yell. I put a finger on my lips and rubbed the fingers of my other hand together, the sign for money. That stopped her. I took out his poke, a fancy leather bag, and threw it to her and told her to open the door. She did. I pulled him in and shut the door.

She spilled the coins out on the bed and yelled, 'The *cabrón*. Look. Ten pesos. But only silver!'

'Hold it. He must have had more. The general is very careful about paying the girls.'

While I talked I was busy pulling off his boots. I figured that they would fit Raul and set them aside for later, after shaking them upside down over the bed. No coins fell out. His gun belt was solid but I used his knife to cut it anyway. Nothing. When I got his vest off, I knew I was right. He had a dozen gold pieces sewed in the lining.

'You can't roll one of General Lara's officers,' she said. But her eyes were bright, and the way she spoke, it came out more of a question than a fact.

'What's your name, honey?'

'Guadalupe.'

'Lupita,' I said, 'here's an eagle.' I flipped her one of the gold pieces.

She had her dress off and was rubbing up against me.

'You take care of him tomorrow when he wakes up, huh, my love?'

'Sure,' I said. 'Hang on now a minute.'

She twisted and moaned. 'Come on, my love. My life. Come with your *mamacita*.'

There for a minute I couldn't remember just why I had come into the room. Then I remembered about the wedding.

'Hold on now! I need a drink.'

And then she grinned up at me. 'You don't need no drink, my big man.' She grabbed my crotch and I couldn't hardly say no, so I said, 'Right. But I'll tie up my friend here and hide him. While you get us a bottle – a couple of bottles of tequila.'

She pouted.

'And then we'll divide the money.'

'Divide the money! *¡Hijo de la gran puta!*' She ran out of the room. She didn't bother even to cover up but ran out bare-assed with nothing but a hotel towel so she was the next thing to being naked. I had no more got the captain rolled under the bed than she came running back in. I had to put my shoulder to the door to hold the soldiers out while she shot a foot-long, inch-thick iron bolt home. They rapped on the door for a while and then wandered off.

'You need a wedding dress and a veil,' I told her.

'*¡Estás loco!*'

'Me, crazy?' I had to laugh, but she was not too far off. Lupita had never before had to put on a wedding dress for a customer. Then she had me by the crotch and it took a lot more will power than I had. I figured we could look for a dress later, but Raul almost broke the door down pounding. Lupita rolled out from under me so quick that I was rutting around on the bed before the message got through.

'Coronel Bliss,' Raul shouted, 'open the door.'

'Go away.' I made a grab for Lupita and fell flat on my face. My pants were not up or down.

'The wedding dress,' Raul shouted. 'The wedding dress.'

'*¡Puta Madre!*' Lupita had a good vocabulary for her trade. 'You really going to marry me?'

'Kind of. We're going to play a joke.'

Lupita giggled. 'I like jokes. Who we going to screw?'

'Lara,' I said.

Lupita sprayed tequila at me. Then she coughed. I pounded her on the back. She slipped and fell to her knees.

'Stop it, you crazy *cabrón.* You got hands as heavy as a burro's balls. You're built like a burro too.' I grinned. She was a bit indelicate, as Gene used to say, but it was a compliment. 'Too bad you're not as smart.'

Now the physical endowments she referred to, if you've ever seen a burro ready to mount a mare in a mule factory, you will realise how that little whore was throwing flowers at me, as the Mexicans call a compliment. But not as smart as a burro! The worst thing you can call a man when you're talking about his thinking ability is a burro. So I clouted her one. She ended up by the door and would have gotten away except Raul was still pounding the door, and when she opened it, without meaning to, he belted her one between the eyes and she went down again.

Raul slipped in and bolted the door again. He had an armful of white lacy cloth.

'Where'd you get the wedding dress?'

'It's a curtain,' he said, 'but I got a lot of pins.'

Lupita was out cold. I got the water pitcher and splashed some water on her. She shook her head. 'That'll be ten pesos, gold,' she said. 'And don't come back. You *revolucionarios* treat a woman like she was a barnyard hen.'

'Yeah,' I said, 'we are that way, but you ain't been pecked yet.'

'Coronel,' Raul said, 'there is no time for you to . . . ah . . . peck her. She's got to get dressed for the wedding.'

'I wish I had stayed on the ranch,' Lupita groaned. 'But I won't play no tricks never on General Lara,' she said. 'I am dumb but not that dumb.'

I dropped a gold piece in front of her.

'No.'

I dropped another and it clinked and so did the others. Pretty soon it was a pile and Lupita kept saying 'No,' but she couldn't look away.

'Come on, Raul,' I said. 'Let's take the money and find another girl. This one's too smart.'

'Give me a drink,' she said. She emptied the bottle and then said, 'How do I get this dress on?'

We had a little trouble dressing her. She kept nipping at the bottle. We had to pin the money into her dress and the weight kept pulling the curtain off. Finally I tore a sheet up and we ran it up from her crotch around her shoulder and pinned it to the leather bag. She clinked a little but she looked pretty good. With the lace mantilla on her head and a piece of curtain wrapped around her face, she could have been Pearl. That is if you were as drunk as Lara had better be.

'Lupita,' I said, 'remember you only speak English.'

'Fuck you.' She smiled. 'I know a lot more,' she said in Spanish.

'Great,' I said. 'You can talk to Pablo Morales.'

'You wait here,' I said. 'If you do a good job, I'll get you another fifty pesos in gold.'

'You're lying to me.'

I took off my stars and gave them to her. 'Here. You keep them. Tomorrow I'll give you the fifty to get them back. A *coronel* even in Lara's army is worth fifty pesos in gold.'

'*'stá bien.*' She was slurring her words a little. She tucked the stars away somewhere.

'Lock the door after us,' I said. 'I'll send for you. Whoever says the preacher is ready, that's the man.'

'What preacher?' she said.

'The one for the wedding.'

'What wedding?'

'Raul,' I said, 'stay with her. I'll send Romero up in a minute.'

The captain was snoring away in the corner where I had dumped him. I picked off the gold bars and took them with me. I found Romero downstairs. He was sitting on the stairs with his boots out in front of him where they could be admired by anyone who was that interested in boots, which was mainly him.

'You are now a captain,' I said.

'What did I do?' Romero asked.

'You are promoted for watching Lupita and bringing her to the wedding. Go on up, first door to the right. And don't lay her. The dress won't take it.'

'With my new boots on?'

'What?'

'I couldn't lay her with my boots on.'

'You could take them off,' I said.

'My new boots!'

'Okay. It was a joke. Just bring her to the wedding. Raul

will tell you what to do.' My head was beginning to hurt so I picked a bottle of tequila off a table and rinsed my throat. It helped.

I took it with me and went to see Pearl. I figured that we could always copper our bet. Gene taught me to always keep another bet going, another bankroll hidden. Even when you get so lucky that a three-card draw will net you a straight flush. So I figured out another bet. Willy said later, when he came to, that for me, it was sheer genius. All I know is that if I had known what it was going to turn into I might have walked all the way to El Paso right then and turned myself in to Sheriff Hollinger to boot.

Romero poked his nose in the door. I yelled at him to get Willy while I kept patting Pearl on the back. I guess I hit her a little too hard because she kicked me in the shins. She rubbed her nose. I had banged it into my chest.

'If you ever marry, Corcho Bliss, you had better get yourself a female grizzly bear.'

'Wait until you're asked,' I said. When she hauled off to swing, I yelled, 'Wait, wait now. Willy! Willy, come on up here.'

Romero and Raul brought Willy in, half carrying him between them. He had a bump on his head big enough to hold his hat up high on his forehead. He also had a wide grin stuck on his skinny face.

'Willy, you better come up with something good or Pearl is going to be Señora Generala Lara.'

'That's good,' Willy said, 'I'll have the same.'

'Willy,' I said. 'Come on. What should we do?'

'Make mine a double,' Willy said.

I snapped my fingers in front of his eyes. He didn't blink, just stared straight ahead, that silly fixed grin stuck on his face.

I sat down on the bed. 'You got a problem,' I told Pearl.

'Ha!' She snorted. 'A problem!'

'Yeah!' I said. 'Who's going to give the bride away?'

That did it. She started to bawl again. I went to pat her on the back and then thought better of it. Raul ripped the end off his shirt, tore it into a rough square, and, with a bow, gave it to Pearl. She blew her nose in it.

'You got any ideas?' I asked.

He shrugged and sat on the bed, head in his hands. So did I. And Pearl. Willy was already there and yet he wasn't. Romero squatted on the floor.

'Why don't she marry the general?' Romero asked.

Before Pearl could scream, I said, 'Now, Romero, the general may be a bit too quick on the trigger and lack a few refinements, but he is a human being and deserves some protection.'

Pearl's mouth snapped open, but just then Willy said, 'Pearl, find the conductor. I think we're on the wrong train.'

She put her arm around him, glared at me and hushed Willy. 'Now, now. We're on the train to El Paso. Don't worry.'

Until Willy got off that train he would be useless, so I decided to go ahead with my own idea.

'Does Lara drink a lot on these happy occasions?' I asked Romero.

'The general always gets drunk when he gets married. Real drunk,' Romero said.

'Falling down, passing out drunk?' I asked.

'Always,' Romero said.

'Do you know the wedding service?' I asked Raul.

'Only the main parts, like "if any person here knows of any reasons why this marriage should not take place, let them speak now or forever hold their peace" and – '

'That's enough,' I said. 'We'll tell Lara that Pearl will only get married in English so she's sure that the hitch is legal.'

'Corcho Bliss, you are a no-good, selfish, cowardly cad.'

'Pearl,' I said, 'don't take on so. The general will be drunk enough by midnight that we can get out of town, grab his horses, and head north. Besides, Raul ain't a priest. He ain't even a Mormon deacon. Are you?'

'Amen,' he said. 'I'll do it' – he batted his eyes at Pearl – 'for Miss Harper's sake.'

We cut a piece off a sheet and wrapped it around Raul's neck until it looked like it might have been a Roman collar.

Then we borrowed Willy's coat and shoes and Captain Raul de la Vega looked just as holy as a drunken missionary, except he had no Bible. Pearl caught that right away.

I sent Romero out. He came back a few minutes later with a small black book. I read the title out loud, '*The Blaster's Handbook.*'

'I thought it was the Bible,' Romero said.

'So will Lara,' I said. 'He can't read Spanish or English.'

I gave the book to Raul. He sat down and began to read, laughing now and then or nodding his head in agreement.

'Pearl,' I said, 'be reasonable!'

'Sure. Marry the Ugly Prince. Maybe he'll turn into a toad.'

'It won't be legal, Pearl,' I said.

'Who'll tell Lara?' she said.

'We'll be gone before he comes to. There just ain't another way.'

'Why do you say "ain't"?'

'Huh?'

'Sometimes you talk as if you had an education and other times you sound like any old-time cowhand.'

'Okay, Pearl,' I said, 'I'll try to do better. Now about this wedding, I assure you – ' I stopped about six words after she said, 'All right. I'll do it.'

'What did you say?'

'I said all right, okay, yes. Bring on the general.'

'You sure you want to, Pearl?'

'Yes!'

I stopped at the door. 'Now, are you dead sure you want to go through with this?'

She grabbed *The Blaster's Handbook* and threw it at me so I guess she meant yes. I went out to get Lara, but something was bothering me. I guessed I needed a drink.

Lara was in a private room at the end of the main floor. A couple of his men were sprawled in front of the door. I stepped over them, but I stopped with my hand on the knob when I heard the hammers on the Colts click back.

'*Cálmense, muchachos.* I just want to tell the general that his bride is ready.'

'What bride?' the one with the laughing shoe-button eyes asked.

'The gringa,' I said.

'That's right,' the other one said. 'My general has been searching the town for a priest.'

'I found a priest,' I said.

'You go in and tell him,' the one with the shoe-button eyes said to his *compañero.*

'Not me, let the gringo tell him. If Lara shoots him we'll know not to go in.'

Shoe Buttons nodded sagely at his comrade's clear thinking. 'Go on in,' he said to me.

I opened the door and shut it quickly behind me. Lara sat in a brocaded chair, his feet up on a dressing table. He had a black look. There were three girls, one of them had clothes on. They all looked scared. Even Pablo seemed worried.

'What do you want, you *cabrón*?' Lara said.

'You talked to me polite last week,' I said.

'Last week you had a gun on, *cabrón*,' Lara said.

Well, he had a point there.

'I found a preacher,' I said.

He jumped to his feet. 'A real one?' He scowled at me. 'Don't try no tricks. I want a real *padre* and a real wedding. I don't fool around with *señoritas*.' He drew himself up. 'I am a very moral man.'

'Sure,' I said. 'I got a real priest, a Bible and Pearl says she's willing to go through with the ceremony if we have a real reception after.'

'What's a reception?' Lara was suspicious.

'A reception is where we have some drinks after the wedding, although a lot of people claim it's better before. In fact most moral people drink a day or so before the wedding and – '

'No,' Lara cut me off. 'I do my big drinking after I get married, not before. What you care when I drink, eh?'

He was suspicious.

'I don't care,' I said. 'As long as I get a drink, I'll even give the bride away.'

Lara grinned then. He ran the girls out. Just as they were. Outside the men cheered. A couple of shots were fired.

'We'll hold the wedding in here,' Lara said.

'Pablo,' I said, 'go get all the *aguardiente* you can find that has a printed label on it. I don't want any homemade poison.'

Lara clapped me on the back. 'You know, gringo, you are a *simpático cabrón*.'

'Dearly beloved, we are gathered here together to join this man and woman in holy matrimony.' Raul was talking too fast. I knew he was afraid he might forget the lines. When I was in the theater I did the same thing.

'These two souls will today be united by God and – '

'Goddamn!' Pablo said. Lara nodded as if he understood.

'Short translation,' I said.

'Where's Pearl?' Willy said.

I handed Willy a new bottle and he went back to his own world. Pearl said out loud, 'Oh, what the hell!' and reached for the bottle. I was getting a little fuzzy too, so I held out my hand for a turn at it. That *aguardiente*, which means 'burning water', was about as big a swallow as I have ever had. It took me a few minutes to get my breath back. I noticed Pearl's eyes were bugged out and she was squinting to see. Later she said she was sure that it was a double wedding.

'The wedding, in deference to the bride . . . ' Raul said, bowed in her direction a little too far, and over he went. Pearl jumped back as his head bounced against the tile floor. Romero and I stood him back up and kind of leaned him against the wall. His thin, white forehead had a big red spot with a white onion on it. His eyes may have been focused on something inside his head for he wasn't seeing much outside.

'Reverend,' I hissed, 'wake up. The wedding.'
'Huh?'
'The wedding!'
'I do!' he said. I shook him a little. Then Romero gave him a shot of that *aguardiente*. Sotol, I think it was.
He blinked. 'Where was I?'
'In deference to the bride,' I said.
'Ah, yes. The wedding will be conducted in English.'
Lara pulled a gun and cocked it.
'With a simultaneous translation by' – I looked around – 'by Coronel Pablo Morales, the only man here with a sufficient command of English to do justice to the words of our reverend. Will you do us the honor, Coronel Morales?'
'*Claro que sí*,' he said. He pulled a gun and leveled it at Raul. 'I'll kill all the bloodsucking priests.'
'No,' I yelled. 'He's a Protestant.'
'Kill them, too,' he said.
'He's got to marry Pearl to the general,' I said. 'You tell the general what he says, Coronel.'
'Why?' Pablo wanted to know.
'Why not?' Lara said.
'*Sí, mi general*.' Pablo saluted. He forgot about the heavy .45 in his hand, so when he rapped his head hard his knees buckled. We sat him up alongside Willy.
'Go ahead,' I said.
Once Raul got into his part he was good. We could have used him as the religious train robber in our theatrical company.
Lara said, '*Vámonos*. Let's go. *Ándale, huevón!*'
'That's no way to talk to a preacher,' I said. 'He's not lazy. It's just that a marriage has got to be done right.'
Lara belched at me. He drank another half a bottle, muttering between swallows.
'Goddamn.' Pablo woke up. 'Fast it or goddamn Pablo will fast it with a goddamn *balazo*.' He drew his Colt automatic and waved it.
'He means hurry up,' I explained to Raul.
'I haven't read from the Bible yet,' Raul complained.

'He hasn't read from the Bible yet,' I said.

'Well, read, *cabrón*, read,' Pablo said in Spanish.

'*Sí*,' Lara yelled, 'read, you *cabrón* preacher, you!'

'All right,' Raul said. He cupped his hands around the Bible but he dropped it. He tried several times to keep his hands holy-looking, but he couldn't hang on to the book. Pablo took out his Colt again so Raul started reading, holding the Bible in one hand. Pablo shoved his Colt back in the holster. It went off and the slug whined around through the room and out a window.

Raul said, 'Quiet, please! Chapter four. Book of Dynamite. Storage. Always keep the dynamite in a dry place for damp dynamite will become unstable, verily, and be exploded, I say unto you, by a slight shock.'

'What he say?' Lara asked.

'The gringas, they get mad like hell,' Pablo said.

'He's telling me,' Lara said. Lara kept edging closer to Pearl. I mean to Lupita. Pearl was crying through her veil.

'And Jehova, Lord of the Hoists, said unto me that a well-tamped charge will do more work than double the powder badly tamped.' He looked up at me sad-faced. He was tired. I guess that I had forgotten how long he had been reading.

'General Lara,' Pablo said from the floor, 'he said that when you crawl on that gringa you better wear your spurs.' He took off his hat and lay down.

I nodded yes at Raul.

'I now pronounce you man and wife!' Raul jumped down from the box and reached for a bottle.

Lara grabbed me. 'You're all right you *gringo cabrón*, you. Drink!'

I drank. Later on I caught Raul's eye and gave him the high sign. Then, while I was waiting, I got to talking to Pearl or maybe it was Lupita and Lara wanted to do the wedding again. I drank to that, and when I got next to Willy, I whispered, 'Right after the wedding.'

'You can't sneeze at a muzzle velocity of eighteen hundred feet per second,' Willy said.

I couldn't argue about that, so I wandered off to look for Pearl, but then I bumped into Lupita and she was so nice I had a drink with her and then Raul helped me up the stairs. I remember, just before I fell asleep, that the staircase had shrunk. It had only one step, although it was a big one. 'I must be growing,' I thought, and went to sleep.

The world was slow in starting. It took more than six days and whoever built it must have had to work nights treading out the adobe with a little straw and some horse manure to give it strength. But when it got going it was something. It rocked and banged and creaked. My eyes wouldn't open. I tried but they were stuck. When I pried one open with my fingers, the pain hit so hard I couldn't breathe. The eye closed when I took my fingers away.

I clapped my hands over my ears but the sound was just as bad inside my head as out. Something lifted me up and whacked me down and I yelled, 'Stop it. Stop. Right now!'

'What did you say, son?'

'Stop!' I fairly well screamed.

'Don't whisper, son. Speak up.'

I got an eye open again and there was Willy bending over me. He was as wavy as a desert mirage and the color of red sandstone.

'How'd you get so red – and stand still, will you?'

'Red? Ah yes. Evidently a filter effect. The . . . ah, red, uh . . . lens covering over your eyes would certainly give objects a pink tinge. So,' he said as an afterthought.

'Red filter. Oh, shit,' I said. 'And what's this "son" bullshit?'

Something cracked me alongside of my head and I almost fainted.

'Pearl,' I said. I knew it had to be Pearl. No one else, not even Pablo, could be so mean ornery as to hit a hungover man in the head.

'Keep a decent tongue in your mouth. There is a lady present.'

'Friend of yours,' I said. I covered my head as quick as I spoke, but I got rapped in the ribs with an ax or maybe a miner's pick. I guess it could have been one of the pointed shoes she wore.

I eased my eyes open again. I was inside some kind of a covered wagon. It was jolting along over a mess of potholes.

'Let me give you a bit of advice, son,' Willy said. 'When you deal with a high-strung lady, such as my daughter, Pearl, think of her as a Morgan mare.' Pearl cocked her left. 'In a manner of speaking, Pearl,' Willy said hastily, 'a blood mare is a high-strung, delicate female to be treated with every consideration. Do you follow me, son?'

'Willy,' I said, 'I do not feel good. I feel bad. Do not call me "son" one more time. And as for you, Miss Morgan . . . I mean Miss Pearl, why don't you help your old man roll me out of this wagon and leave me to die alongside of the road. Maybe a band of Apache Indians will wander by. They, being a humane people, will maybe only roast me over a slow fire.'

Pearl said, 'Sure,' and started shoving.

'No,' Willy said. 'Wait up!' He made a quick draw from a shoulder holster and brought out a flask. I retched.

'Hold your nose,' Willy said.

I did. I got down one big shot and then just hung on.

'Where are we?'

'About ten miles out of Chihuahua, west and north.'

'Where's Lara?'

'Looking for us.'

I sat all the way up. 'Lara can drink more than I thought. But I guess we got him drunk enough. So he married Lupita, eh?'

'There was a little problem there,' Willy said. 'Do you remember I recovered my, uh, equilibrium just as Raul passed out?'

'No.'

'I thought not,' Willy said. 'At this point Pablo found a regular priest hiding in a closet.'

I felt better and took another swig.

'So old Lara got hitched legal like. Aha!'

'Yes, that he did,' Willy said. 'You don't remember your part in the ceremony?'

'My part?'

'Yes.' Pearl had the meanest grin. 'Your part,' she said. 'Let me present myself. I am Mrs. Pearl Bliss, wife of that great matchmaker and drunk, Corcho Bliss.'

'Willy,' I said, 'can I have that flask back?' I took a deep one and in a minute of two I spoke quietly. 'Now, Pearl, let us try one more time. What are you trying to say?'

'That we got married last night, you drunken idiot!'

Enough was enough. 'Wait a minute. Just one goddamn minute. Stop this prairie schooner a minute. Whoa!' I yelled, and I heard Romero call out something and then Raul translated and the wagon stopped. It felt pretty good until Willy said, 'Well, son?'

'Stop that! I thought you didn't care for heavy drinking,' I said to Pearl.

She turned red. 'I don't.'

'Well,' I wanted to know, 'is it just me that got married?'

'No,' she said, 'we both got married.'

'Well then, I guess you said yes.' I had her there and I knew it. She was squirming too. I almost felt sorry for her until Willy said, 'Lara was pretty drunk, too. He figured that you had wronged a nice Mexican girl, Lupita – he meant Pearl.' Willy coughed and looked down at his shirt front. 'Lara said if you didn't marry her, he'd blow your head off. So you said you would.'

'And Pearl?'

'Pearl said "no" for Lupita, then Lara said he'd shoot you so Pearl said she would and you agreed and there you are.'

'But that's not legal,' I said. 'The license or whatever has got me married to Guadalupe Sánchez or something.'

'No,' Pearl said quietly.

'Why'd you do that?' I said. 'Haven't I got trouble enough?'

'Because I was dying to be the wife of that great and adorable gentleman, Corcho Bliss,' Pearl yelled. I flinched, but she didn't hit me.

'You feeling all right,' Pearl?' I asked.

She started to bawl.

'Aw, come on, Pearl,' I said. 'It don't count anymore than a busted straight against four hearts. You was probably too drunk to write another name.'

'Get out. Go away. Live with the Apaches!'

'That may be prophetic,' Willy said.

Dust was growing off to our left maybe five miles. It might have been wild horses except the dust was running just about right to cut us off in a half an hour or so.

'What guns we got?'

Willy shook his head.

'None?'

He didn't answer.

'What horses?'

'Just the one we took from Raul.'

'Raul,' I yelled, 'will she run?'

'Yes, she will.'

'All right, Pearl,' I said, 'you mount up and don't stop till you hit El Paso.'

'No,' Pearl said, 'I'll take my chances with you. All of you.'

'Pearl,' I said, 'what chance?'

That did it. She whimpered a little and then clamped her jaw shut and shook her head. She was stubborn.

'Pearl,' Willy said, 'Corcho could tell you what the Indians will do to you.'

'I'll do better,' I said. 'When they get close enough, I'll kill you myself.'

'You wouldn't,' she said, wide-eyed. I never said another word. She swallowed. She looked at Willy. He nodded.

'All right. As soon as we're ready I'll ride away.' Tears were running down her cheeks but her voice was steady.

I eased out the front of the wagon, between Romero and Raul. 'What do you figure?'

'Apaches,' said Romero.

Raul said, 'I can't see.'

Romero said, 'They're Apaches.'

I squinted and through a cloud of dust I saw a file of riders. I couldn't see any saddles but I couldn't believe there were still wild Apaches out raiding.

'Right,' I said. I ducked back in.

'Willy,' I said, proud of myself, 'I got a plan.'

'Corcho, if you forget it, I will.'

'No, Willy. This one will maybe save us. At least some of us,' I added. My hands and knees were starting to shake. When that happened I was about ready to fight and I was also as scared as I could get. It would stop when I got into the real thing.

'You and Pearl peel off here. Take Raul's horse and bear off north and east. Just before we come up with the Apaches, I'll whip up the team and we three will jump and make for the hills. We'll meet in El Paso at the bank, Mondays at noon.'

Pearl said, 'No. You'll never make it. Let's stay together. Maybe if we give them the team.'

'That would be like playing poker for beans,' I said. 'No fun at all to a growing Apache boy. Go on, git.'

'Come on, Pearl,' Willy said.

'Corcho Bliss, you are a lot of things and one of them is a man.' Pearl gave me a kiss that would have stopped a railroad watch. Close up like that Lupita wasn't near as cushiony. I wondered what it would be like to be married to Pearl. Willy yanked at her and she jumped, the reins of Raul's fast mare in her hand. Willy squeezed my shoulder and went after her.

Raul had filled Romero in so he knew what was up.

'These aren't bad horses,' Romero said. 'If they were not pulling a wagon, they might go pretty fast.'

'There are three of us,' Raul said.

'Odd man out,' I said.

They both nodded. I called one, two, three and we each brought out one hand from behind our back. I had two fingers up. So did Raul. So did Romero. 'One more time,' I said and we repeated. This time I had one. So did Romero. Raul had two. He nodded and said, 'It has been a pleasure. The bank at noon, any Monday.' He jumped.

'Shall we give them a real chase?' I asked Romero.

'Why not?' he said. He never seemed to care much whether he lived or died, but I had learned a long time ago that a man inside is about like another when it comes to hurting and scaring.

We climbed out on the horses. Romero had a knife. He pantomimed cutting the harness and then throwing the knife to me. I nodded and whacked the off horse, mine, on the rump with my hat. They broke into a trot, then a gallop. There wasn't enough of a trail for a run. Off to our left, between us and the mountains, the dust was bigger and closer. It pulled closer and closer until I could see feathers and then the war party, maybe a dozen riders, pulled alongside and paced us. Romero pointed to our left. Almost hidden a deep dry wash ran alongside the trail.

'Let's go,' I yelled.

Romero cut his traces and, keeping his horse in step, tossed me the knife. I caught it by the handle and cut my horse loose. I had already rolled the reins up over my hand so I just had to yank that big horse around and kick it into the brush, right angles to the dry wash. Romero caught the idea right away. They would have to ride a ways to cross that wash, then come back, and then pick up the trail. It would give us maybe five minutes.

Not much. But then how do you measure time? Talk to a man with his back to the wall and ask him if he'd rather have a cigar than a cigarette for his last smoke.

The cactus and brush cut us and the horses. I had my arm over my eyes and my hat brim clamped under it. Still, I could see the ground. When we hit a game trail I yanked back and to the left and then my gelding was on to it. We still got cut up, but we were making better time.

Something flicked my shoulder. It was Romero with a rein end. He pointed at himself so I pulled over and he went pounding by. He knew this country and for the first time I thought that we might have a chance. Then I saw the first mustang through the screen of brush and my heart came up to turn my mouth to brass.

It wasn't more than three minutes until they cut that game trail, but it gave us a two-mile lead. I sure hoped Romero knew where he was headed, because I knew those little Indian braves could run their ponies through that brushy trail as fast as the jack rabbits made it to begin with.

Suddenly the spiny branches stopped whipping into me. I lifted my left arm up and peeked under it. We had turned off on to a passable wagon road. This helped a little. Our buggy horses were not fast but they could run along pretty well on a decent road. Not that we could outrun the Indian mustangs, but we could draw the war party a long way away from Pearl, although why I wanted to do that I couldn't figure out. Maybe it was my new status. Being married and all. That jolted me awake. I was able to rein alongside Romero and I yelled, 'Are those real Indians?'

'Mostly.'

'Mostly what?'

'Mostly Indians.'

I figured that could go on for a while so I asked, 'Look, I heard there are some renegade Apaches up in the hills still but they don't come down to raid, so what are these?'

'Bandits.'

'*¿Revolucionarios?*'

'No, just bandits. Some Apaches and Mexicans raised Apache and some *pistoleros*. They just as soon kill a *revolucionario* as a Federalista.'

'They're wearing feathers,' I said.

'That's their uniform,' Romero yelled. 'A wild turkey feather stuck in their hatband.'

I looked back and saw a horse break out on the wagon trail, slide to its haunches and then break into a quick run after us. I started to whip a rein to my horse but Romero made the 'no' sign, his finger waving back and forth like a railroad semaphore signal. 'We run these horses they catch us for sure in five minutes; we lope, maybe we get away.'

He was right. The timing, as we used to say in the theater, was not good. If we ran our buggy horses, they would give out in a couple of miles and they would have us. If we loped along, we could outrun them unless they put on a sprint and caught us, which, I found out by looking back over my shoulder, they were doing.

Romero looked back to. His deep-brown face had a pale look to it for a second.

'Anyway' – I figured I'd comfort him – 'they ain't Apaches.'

'No,' Romero said, 'they're worse.'

We pounded along at a steady lope, listening to the hoof-beats getting louder and, when the road straightened, getting a good look at the riders. And every time they were getting bigger. From jack-rabbit size to coyotes and then wolf size and getting closer. Romero held up three fingers and I read his sign. Only three horses were still running. The rest had dropped out of the race. A man without a spare horse might just as well shoot himself in this country if he ruined the one he was riding.

On the next straight stretch another one dropped out, but the two left were within range now and worn rifle barrels flashed in the sun. They both fired at the same time. That didn't scare me. Shooting from horseback at a moving target is useless. They knew it too, I figured, but they thought we might just pull up, or run our horses hard to get out of range and then, when our horses tired, their riders would sprint a few seconds to pick us up. They were moving closer though and a man with a rifle can hit a target, moving or otherwise, if he's got his rifle barrel a couple of feet from your back.

The first man was fifty yards away when his horse stumbled and went down. The rider came down with him and then we turned a bend. The second horse had closed to about thirty yards when its rider pulled a fancy trick. He stopped his pony, as quick as any top roping horse, was out of the saddle before the horse had stopped, and, as cool as a man hunting deer, he swung his rifle up and shot Romero out of the saddle. The next shot sounded funny to me because I was hanging on to the mane of my mount when I heard it. I guess I was hit before I could hear the shot. When I turned to look for Romero, I heard another shot. This one took the buggy horse in the right flank and he broke into a run. My eyes took a picture that I could look at whenever I wanted, though. Romero was laying there in the middle of the wagon track, not moving. The nasty young man that I thought was dead had a fancy hat with a feather in it. Gene's young poker-playing friend who liked to think he was Billy the Kid had killed Romero and maybe Corcho Bliss. And maybe not. My horse was not hit bad and I wanted to see the kid again. I had gotten to like Romero. Blood was seeping through my shirt high on the left side. I couldn't untwine my hands from the long black hair for I was afraid I'd just slide off, so I let the horse gallop on.

The chaparral alongside the trail gave way to scrub oak, then the scrub oak started to get wavy and change shape. I lost track of time, but once I almost fell and when I jerked myself back on the buggy horse, its back was slippery with blood. The horse was walking now. I tried to turn to see my back trail and couldn't, but I couldn't hear anything. Then I fell into a big black pit and someone down there hit me one alongside the head and pinched my nose hard. I got one flash and I couldn't see anything but the bright sun, and then the curtain came down and the act was over. Just before I went out I wondered if I'd get a curtain call.

Somehow I had got to be a maverick calf and a couple of bush poppers had me in between them, swinging short loops, low to keep them out of the bush, but the mesquite was too thick and I figured to make it when one of the riders, it was Billy, made a grab for my tail, took a turn around his boot and pulled up short. I went headfirst into the ground. Pablo came running in and hog-tied my front left foot to my hind right. Billy was cackling away, that old picture of Billy the Kid in one hand and a red-hot branding iron in the other. Just before he shoved the iron down at me I kicked hard and mooed the best I could but he kept coming. I rolled my eyes to see the iron. It was a big C.S. My own brand.

I screamed and arched up off the ground. My ribs were burning. Legs and skirts were flying through the air. I must have thrown a couple of the *soldaderas* at least six feet. Carmencita, Tex's never-faithful ex-wife, had a half-empty bottle in her hand. I sat up and checked my wound. What looked like a bloody rope burn cut across my left side just under the rib cage.

'Give me a shot of that tequila, Carmencita!'

'It's sotol.' Why does a woman, white, brown, or black, have to be so contrary?

'It's all the same,' I said. 'Give!'

I took a big swallow. Then I gagged. Then I coughed. I dropped the bottle and beat at the ground until I could breathe. Someone handed me an *olla* full of water. I drank that. Or most of it.

'Want another shot?' Carmencita had picked up the bottle.

'Save it to start fires with.'

'Okay.' She started to put it away.

'Hang on. Let's see it.' I took just a couple of drops. It burned all the way down, but it got me on my feet. 'How'd you find me?'

'The dogs smelled you. We got here before they decided to eat you.'

'I do smell pretty ripe. Where's the camp?'

'Over there.' Carmencita pointed west.

'See you later,' I said. I started back down the trail, east. But my legs turned on me and I had to sit down.

'You're going the wrong way,' Carmencita said. 'The camp is just over the hill. You come with me. By the time the men get back, you'll be fine.'

'The men get back?'

'Those *cabrones.* They left some of us here. The general, that *cabrón,* he took that blond *puta* along with him and left me here. With the old women and the kids.' She yelled at one of the women I had kicked into a scrub oak to help and I leaned on them and hobbled into camp.

The camp was deserted except for a dozen women, all old except for Carmencita, and about a hundred kids. There may have been only fifteen or twenty, but they moved so fast I could have counted the same one three or four times. There were also chickens, pigs and burros, but not one horse.

'Where's the horses?'

'With the cavalry, where else?'

'Sure. Where else. Don't we even have one for, say, to bring wood in?'

'You better have some more sotol,' Carmencita said. 'Wood is one thing we're not short of.' We were in a clearing in a pine forest.

She put me in a hut on a blanket spread over a straw *petate* on the floor. A saddle slipped in behind me let me sit up enough to eat. I got down a dozen tortillas laced with chili and a couple of bowls of black beans and *epazote.* The sotol chased with ice-cold river water wasn't so bad and I slept again.

When I woke up, it was cold. Half asleep still, I saw a bundle of blankets alongside me. They were all tangled up, and before I knew what they were tangled with, I had Carmencita in bed with me.

She cuddled right up and before I knew it I was sweating. Both of us with our clothes still on.

'You change partners pretty fast, don't you?' I was awake now and remembering the gambler called Tex.

'What else is there?' she said.

Yeah. What else was there. She had probably lost three or four 'Juanes' in fights with the Federales by now, so what was another man except some protection and food.

I slipped my hand under her skirt. The flesh was so firm you couldn't have dented it with a ball peen hammer. She closed her legs tight and pushed my hand with both hers.

'You take me away from here with you?'

'On foot?'

'I got a horse.' That explained the saddle I was using as a pillow.

'Two on one horse. We'd never make it.'

'Four hours away, we buy another horse.'

'I got no money.'

'You take me and we get plenty of money. Then we buy horses and we go far away. We live together or apart. No difference.'

'Where do you get all this money?'

'I got Tex's map. It was sewed into the saddle you're sleeping on.'

Tex's map. The tower! 'Let's see it.' I was interested now. It seemed more real if tough little Carmencita believed in it.

'When we get there,' she said.

'When do we leave?' I asked.

'Early in the morning.' Her voice got huskier. 'You want to sleep or . . . ' She left it at that but her legs relaxed and she guided my hand with hers.

'Let's or first,' I said.

At dawn we wandered out of camp. Earlier I had carried the saddle and bridle through the sleeping camp and dropped it in some brush off the trail. There was a little rabbit trail leading off the main trail and we followed it, me with the saddle. My side hurt to beat hell, but otherwise I felt good. Carmencita went up the trail like a plump fawn. She was smiling and excited. Being used to a man or maybe men around and then being cut off must have been bad for her blood. The air was still icy from the night, but I was sweating when we reached a tiny meadow. A mustang was pegged there. I dumped the saddle, then sat on it. It took me a while to catch my breath.

"You getting old, Corcho?' Carmencita giggled.

'Another night like last one and that horse won't even feel my weight.' I was a few years older than Carmen. Hell. A few. More like twenty. She couldn't be over twenty-five.

'How old are you, Carmencita?' I eased the saddle blanket on the horse, a coyote-colored gelding, and then swung the saddle up.

'Eighteen,' she said.

Eighteen! 'How many, uh, husbands you had, Carmencita?'

'Four that I stayed with long enough to count.'

I tightened up the cinch. When the mustang relaxed I kneed him in the belly and yanked hard on the cinch. He wouldn't slip the saddle on me now.

'Let's go,' Carmencita said. 'That Lara find us and we'd better cut our own throats.' She had our only weapon, a butcher knife.

'Who cuts first?' I asked.

'I'll cut yours for you,' Carmencita offered. 'You gringos don't use knives too well.'

'Thanks.'

'*De nada*.' She smiled. She really meant it. Well, maybe if Pablo was about to get his hands on me, the favor would be appreciated.

We took turns riding up the trail. The sun was at about ten o'clock when Carmencita called a halt. She pointed up ahead. 'That's the keyhole,' she said.

There was a big rock cliff and the wind and rain had cut

through the rock in a way I had never seen before, not even in southern Utah, where there are the oddest rocks I had ever seen before this one.

The hole at the top was bigger than the one at the bottom and it did look like a keyhole. Most names don't fit but this one did. At least I've never seen a mesa that looked like a table or a rainbow bridge that didn't look like an old crumbling pile of stone.

'Let's go.'

Carmencita hung back. 'There's only the one way in according to the map.'

I got her point. 'How far in?'

'I can't read.'

'Give me the map.'

She hung back. 'You will take me with you? You won't leave me?'

'Of course not. We don't have enough blankets for these cold nights. Give me the map.'

She had the damned thing pinned up in her hair. Luckily it was folded four times and her natural hair oil hadn't gotten to the inside.

Tex had been an educated man. Most gamblers were. He had marked a scale in miles on the map. The tower should be less than a mile inside and a cave at the base of the tower was marked with an X. Alongside, Tex had written '$1,000,000.00'

'I wish I could cut you in, partner,' I said out loud.

'*¿Que?*' Carmencita asked.

'Nothing,' I said. 'You wait here. You can see the trail for a mile below. If you see anyone, sing out. I'll hear you and come running.'

I looked up the trail. It was narrow and rough over loose rock. We couldn't risk an injured horse. 'I'll pick up enough to see us out. We can come back later for more.'

'Corcho, can you carry back as much as one thousand pesos?'

'Sure,' I said. 'Easy that much.'

'Ay! I'll be rich. Hurry.'

I handed her the reins.

It was tough climbing up through the keyhole. For every two steps I made up I slipped back one. Inside the keyhole the trail leveled out and turned. Up ahead, no more than three-quarters of a mile, a rock tower leaned up against the high cliffs. Lara was a smart man. The valley was rimmed by cliffs that a six-legged mountain sheep couldn't climb. There was only one way in, and out.

With that pleasant thought I heard a gunshot. I tore back through the opening, took me a big jump, lit on my feet and rolled down that shale slope right into a file of riders. Up ahead I could hear the clatter of horseshoes against the rocky trail.

Pablo grinned down at me.

'Coronel Bliss!' He looked up at the sky. 'Thank you, God, I promise you that the next time I shoot a priest I give him an extra-long start.' He pointed at me. 'Tie him on a horse.'

My insides were as cold as a mountain stream.

'And Carmencita?' I asked.

'So that was the *puta*. She is small, weighs about as much as a boy.' He closed his eyes, then asked, 'She's got a coyote mustang?'

'Yes.'

'That's a good horse. She's light. She may get away. She had a good start.'

'How good?' I asked.

'About five minutes,' Pablo said.

Then I was over a saddle, tied hands to feet, watching the ground go by.

A five-minute start. I couldn't decide whether I wanted Pablo's man to catch Carmencita or not.

The sun was almost overhead when they dumped me off the packhorse on to the dirt patio of a ruined ranch house. By rubbing my legs and hands together I got a little feeling back before they tied me again hands to feet. Pablo was taking no chances.

'Coronel! Hey, Coronel Bliss!'

It was Raul.

'How did they catch you, Raul?'

Raul was tied like me. He rolled over, his nose almost touching his knees.

'I am not a very brave nor a stoic man, Coronel. My nose betrayed me. I, who would never think of less than three wines with a seven-course dinner, smelled beans cooking and my traitorous nose led me right into this camp of *revolucionarios*.'

'Raul,' I said, 'I wish you were in New Orleans right now ordering one of those seven-course dinners.'

'And you, Coronel?' Raul asked.

'In this dream I am sitting across from you,' I said, 'checking the wine list.'

'Done,' Raul said. 'As soon as we have done with this place, I'll invite you.' He dropped his eyes. 'I have ample funds in other countries.'

I'll bet he did. The was one of Mexico's problems. Everybody had money somewhere else. And they spent it someplace else, too.

'We'll never make it, Raul,' I said. 'They'll shoot us.'

'Us?' Raul said. 'That's a lot of people.'

'And how might you get out?'

'I shall, as a recently ordained minister, appeal to their innate sense of decency – '

'Hah!' I grunted.

'And as a slight added inducement I shall offer them five thousand pesos in gold.'

'That may work for you,' I said, 'but not for me.'

'But my friend, a life for a life. I owe you one, so my offer is good only for the two of us.'

'Forget me, Raul,' I said. 'Thanks, but after Pablo caught me nosing around the tower, I'm as good as dead.'

'The tower?'

'Lara piles his loot in a hidden cave at the base of a mountain called the tower.'

'A treasure?'

'The man who told me – he's deader than me – claimed there is at least a million dollars in that cave.'

'All the better. You can pay me back. They have my offer and I just added another five thousand for you.'

'They will damned well shoot me,' I said. 'Why Pablo hasn't before, unless he's got some Indian tricks for me, I don't understand.'

'My *coronel*, Don Pablo, wants you. Over by the corral. Both of you.'

I had just enough slack in my hands-and-feet tie to hobble along.

'Five will get you two, Raul, that *amigo* Pablo has not invited us to dinner.'

'New Orleans, Corcho. At my invitation.'

'Shut up,' our guide said. 'My *coronel* does not like to wait.' He helped us along with a few pretty expert kicks. Our ropes let us shuffle along like a couple of short-hobbled horses over to a slick-pole corral.

Pablo sat at a big round table that must have been taken out of the dining room of the hacienda. About fifty yards to his right there was a six-foot-high adobe wall. To his left there were about two hundred men.

Pablo had four Colt single-action revolvers laid out on

the table in front of him. A tin bucket was filled with fat round-nosed .45 loads. A young soldier stood by his side. The prisoners' hands were tied and their feet hobbled.

'What do you plan to do?' I asked. 'Shoot them all?'

The young soldier laughed, then the guards laughed. The prisoners didn't laugh but I saw one grin as if his boss had told him a joke he didn't understand.

'Maybe,' Pablo said. 'Let the first one go.'

The man who had grinned, by the look of him a pureblood Indian, wore a white shirt with the tails tied around his waist and white pants loose around the crotch to let the air circulate. He still grinned.

Pablo said, 'Make them jump around a minute. Let a dozen loose at a time. I don't want any that can't run.'

The Indian moved around a little, still grinning.

'If you make it over the wall,' Pablo said, 'I let you go.'

'And if I don't?' The Indian spoke with the Chinese sing-song dialect of the hills and his Spanish wasn't any better than that of a Texas trail cook.

'It won't matter to you,' Pablo said.

He got it then. 'You going to shoot me.'

Pablo just nodded.

The Indian measured the distance. He could have been calculating the length of a *maíz* furrow.

'Where do I start from?'

Pablo motioned with a revolver. There was a stake about thirty yards in front of the table. The Indian looked at me. I gave him a sign with my head that meant 'watch me' to the Utes. I don't know if he got it or not, but if he didn't, it worked out anyway.

'Pablo,' I said, 'the general wants soldiers.'

'Not these. They've been traded too much.'

'You are a miserable cowardly son of a bitch,' I said.

He spun out of his chair and kicked. I was waiting so he got me on the leg. I couldn't move much, what with my hands tied in back and then on down to the hobbles. He swung the cocked gun at my head. I fell back and he missed. He pointed the gun at me and fired. My eyes froze open but the pain flooded into my head and I could hear all the little sounds that you hear when you are either six years old or about to die. I guess my face went scared too. It was enough to make Pablo laugh.

He pointed the gun again. This time I was looking down the barrel. I couldn't shut my eyes.

'No!' I cried out.

Pablo laughed out loud.

'Don Pablo! The prisoner!'

'What?' He whirled and shot, but a white form flashed over the wall.

'Indian!' he yelled. '*¡Pinche Indio! ¡Siempre traicionan!*' He was mad because the Indian double-crossed him. 'If a man tries to leave before I say go, shoot him.'

A rifleman pulled the hammer back on his Winchester, his teeth flashing white against his brown skin. '*Sí, mi coronel.*'

'Raul,' I asked, 'am I bad hit?'

'No. He just shot a piece of your ear off. You have more than enough left.'

'Enough for what?' I asked. 'Will I need a piece of an ear in a few minutes?'

'He can't kill you until Lara comes back,' Raul said.

'Until Lara comes back,' I repeated. 'How do you know?'

'Because Pablo is supposed to get you killed in battle . . . with witnesses. General Castillo, he'll see you die in battle.'

'That sounds interesting.' It didn't much, but anything was better than dying right now.

'You will be leading a charge. They will talk about it years from now. A suicide charge against a Federal machine gun. A glorious cavalry charge.'

'I know I ain't bright, but who'd follow anybody into that kind of a dead end?'

'I will,' Raul said, 'and so will about fifty prisoners. That is if Pablo doesn't kill them all.'

I hunched a shoulder against my ear to stop the bleeding. Pablo held a cocked Colt revolver in his right hand. He called out '*Uno.*'

The skinny brown man in the baggy white pants didn't get

halfway to the wall before Pablo shot the back of his head off.

'Next,' he yelled. The same man except without a bloody pulp for a head made it to the wall. The third died clawing at the adobe. So did the next. Then I saw that Pablo was holding his shots until they made the wall and then, just as they started up and over to life, he placed a bullet between their shoulder blades.

I shut my eyes. Still shots rang out. Pablo chuckled occasionally. I had never heard him laugh before except when Lara said something that was supposed to be funny. Pablo just did it because he thought Lara was God. He wasn't afraid of him as a man. He just did whatever Lara said or what he thought he wanted.

After a few more shots I opened my eyes and watched Pablo stop another man with his hands pulling at the top of the wall. He slid back down leaving a bright-red streak on the yellow adobe.

'I'm tired of shooting these Indians. Their legs are too short.' Pablo sounded like a thirsty cowboy in a Mormon settlement.

A flat-faced soldier with yellow eyes and a wide grin pointed a cocked rifle at me.

'That gringo. He's got the longest legs of anyone. He could jump the wall, maybe.'

Pablo grinned. It was his kind of a joke. 'Sure,' he said. 'Why not?'

The corporal yanked a machete out of his waistband and slashed down. I spread my legs and shut my eyes. He was good. He didn't even nick my boots. I soon found out why.

'Can I have the boots?' he asked.

'Why not?' Pablo said.

The corporal dropped his machete and pulled on a boot.

'Not yet,' Pablo yelled. 'Let a man die with his boots on, will you?'

The corporal tried to get the boot back on. I kicked him in the chest with my free foot and he and boot flew back into the prisoners. One of them kicked him in the head. He just lay there.

Pablo nodded his head and a soldier with good shoes, a captain at least, sawed away at my wrists and occasionally at the ropes until I could break the strands loose.

'Lara will not like this,' Raul said. 'He will come back and say Pablo did not do as he was told. That is what he will say. What he will do,' Raul said piously, 'only God knows.'

'You are a talker,' Pablo said. 'I wonder if your legs move as fast as your mouth.'

'Hold on, Pablo,' I said.

Pablo got up from the table.

'He is a gringo and can be excused because he is what he is. Nothing. But you are a Mexican. An officer in the old army. You can read and write.' Then he screamed, 'A Mexican! I shit in the milk of your mother. You have no mother. You fairy *cabrón*!'

Raul was pale. He turned almost transparent. Pablo walked up to me and pointed a cocked revolver at my head.

'My General Lara is not here. Only Pablo is here. You want to save your friend? Just say "shoot me". That's all. Then I shoot you and I let Raul go. Okay, *gringo cabrón*. Go ahead. Tell it to me. Say it.'

His eyes were blank with nothing in them. His tongue kept licking at his mustache. He meant it all right. About me talking.

I shook my head for no and said nothing. I could smell his hate and my fear. I could taste my fear, cold and brass-like in my mouth.

'No,' I said. 'I'll run for it but I don't want to die with no go for it at all.'

'And you, my *manso* Mexican?' he asked Raul. *Manso*, the way he put it, meant, at its best, a tame petlike animal. And Raul, who didn't like to fight and could use a gun hardly, said, 'Why not? I owe him a life and my family pays its debts.'

'Raul,' I started to yell, 'he ain't fooling. He's mad, Raul.'

But Raul never heard anything except a loud sound from a Colt .45. If he heard that. I like to think my thought got to him before Pablo's slug splattered his brains over me.

I started for Pablo, but my legs didn't have enough blood and I went down. I felt the muzzle then touch my neck and a great calm came over me. I knew then just what a Mexican means, and not even an Apache can die better, when he says, 'If they're going to kill me tomorrow, why not today?'

'Shoot,' I said. 'It's the only way you'd ever get me, you bandy-legged, long-nosed, slab-sided son of a Digger Indian's outcast dog.'

I heard the click of the hammer being released. He wasn't going to shoot me. Not right then.

'Get up.'

I got up slowly. Pablo was smiling. 'You cuss pretty good.' He turned to the corporal, who was moaning and holding his belly where I had kicked him.

'Bury that one.' He pointed to Raul. 'With his boots on. He wasn't so *manso*.'

The corporal was still a little somewhere else and he started to pull a boot off Raul.

'No,' Pablo said. 'Leave the boots. And,' he said as the corporal picked up a shovel, 'dig an extra grave.'

The corporal nodded. He turned and moved off, then stopped and said very softly, 'A large grave, my *coronel*?'

'No,' Pablo said, measuring him with his eyes, 'a small one. About the length of your shovel.'

The corporal's eyes lifted slowly until he looked up at the top of the long-handled shovel. It reached the tip of his coarse, black hair. Just his size. Someone with shoes on shoved him away and in a minute he was busy digging away in the dry sandy soil. For a minute I thought he was going to whistle.

'Lara won't be happy with you, Pablito,' I said. Pablito! Little cute Pablo. I used the *tú* form, which is either a sign of friendship or an insult. Pablo knew I didn't like him that much so he laid his gun barrel along my head.

I sat down. Just then Lara and about a dozen of his bodyguards rode up. They had a wagon and six prisoners bouncing along in it. They all had ties but one. He looked clean, but poor.

Lara swung off his horse. He toed Raul's head over to see who he was. He looked at me.

'A few seconds more and Pablo would have sent me along with Raul.'

Pablo stood still.

Lara cocked his head at Pablo.

'Against my orders!'

'Yes, my general.'

'One day, Pablo, I'll have you shot.'

'I'll do it for you,' I said.

'You give the order, my general, and I'll do it myself,' Pablo said. He thumbed the hammer back on his .44 and touched his right eyebrow with the muzzle.

'*Ay, ¡que Pablo!*' Lara said. I had an aunt once who used to scold me the same way for tracking manure in the kitchen.

Without looking at me, Lara said, 'We need some money. These city men, they have some. After we persuade them to contribute to the revolution, you can shoot the gringo.'

'But how about General Roble? He will be angry.'

'*Chingue a su madre al General Roble,*' Lara snapped. 'The *cabrón* turned against me.'

Pablo's jaw dropped. 'He's going against you!'

'That's right. Against me. Also against Uribe and Trejo.'

Pablo took his hat off. 'Well, at least we have Calderón with us and he's the best of the bunch.'

'He's not with us either,' Lara said. He put his arm around Pablo. 'Just us. Like old times. You and me and the boys against the *pinches rurales*.'

'We'll show them,' Pablo said.

'We will! Now let's see our benefactors. Sign them up over here,' Lara ordered.

They ranged in color of hair and eyes from light to dark, but to a man their faces were white. Lara started with the first man in line. Black suit and tie. Fat white face. Collar stained wet with sweat.

'How much can you give to the revolution, *mi excelente señor*?' Lara said, being flowery.

'Well, you know that I really wish to give all that I can spare, deprive my family of certain items we have previously enjoyed, to help you, General Lara, whom I have heard called the Napoleon of the West.'

He tittered, then stopped cold when Lara didn't change expression.

'All I can afford,' he said weakly.

'How much? In gold,' Lara said.

'Two hundred gold – ' He stopped short. 'Three hundred gold pesos. I will have to sacrifice, but the revolution comes first.'

Lara looked him in the eye for a moment. Then he moved a step. They all reacted the same except for the last man. He was a bewildered little man with gray eyes, the one without a tie. He looked agreeable and seemed to say '*I like you, why don't you like me? Let's be friends.*'

'And how much can you give?' Lara asked.

'Whatever I have, which is maybe ten pesos in gold if my wife hasn't taken any from the *olla* since last week.'

'*¡Hijo de la gran puta!*' Lara slapped his hip. 'You're all alike. All of you rich merchants. Lies, all lies. We know you have money and we know about how much. You. Again. How much?'

'But General Lara, these gentlemen are bankers and lawyers, while I sell milk from my four cows. I have eight children – '

'String him up,' Lara ordered.

'No! I can pay no more. No!'

His voice was choked off by a rough noose. One end had been tossed over a scrub oak and he was jerked up to his toes. His fingers dug at the noose.

'Let him down,' Lara said. 'Loosen the knot.'

Lara put an arm around the man. 'Look, milkman,' Lara said, 'we want to help you. We don't want to hurt you. We know you got a lot more.'

He just shook his head, his eyes rolling around like a spooked horse.

Lara jerked his thumb up.

The milkman gurgled and tried to climb the rope.

A thin frightened man stepped forward and said, his voice low, 'I beg your pardon, General Lara, but what the man says is true. He has no money.'

'Do you want to take his place?' Lara barked.

'No,' the man said. 'No. Not at all.' He stepped back into line.

'Let him down,' Lara said.

Pablo's long nose twitched. Maybe he could smell death, and of course when the body lets go like that at a hanging, it's not difficult to smell. 'I think he's dead.'

Lara kicked the corpse. 'You're right, Pablo. A man that loved money more than life.' He turned to face the five remaining city men. 'I will send a messenger to town to collect. I know how much to ask for, but I want to see who the true patriots are. If I do not get the money by sundown, some of you will have necks like swans.'

Pablo stuck a thick forefinger in the first man's chest. 'How much?'

'Two thousand . . . please, it's all I can get . . . but I have furniture, horses.'

'Bring the horses. Next.'

In five minutes they had pledged $18,000 in gold. Lara didn't question their answers. He sent them off.

Pablo said, 'I don't think the milkman had any money, my general.'

Lara said, 'I know he didn't. That's why we brought him along. We couldn't kill a rich man and lose his money, could we?'

Pablo stared at Lara. 'You are a genius,' Pablo said. 'Napoleon never, in a million years, could have done it.' Pablo pinched his nose. Wide-eyed he said, 'And he never had the money! He must have been one confused milkman!' Pablo started to laugh. Then he hooted and hollered and Lara laughed and said that the idea had just come to him that morning and Pablo said it was the best he ever heard and Lara said it was pretty good at that. Then suddenly Pablo remembered me. He grinned.

'I kill the gringo then?'

'General Castillo is still backing us and he liked the gringo.'

'I found him right by the tower. The wife of the other gringo, the dead one, uh, Carmencita, was with him.'

'Where is the little whore?' Lara asked. In a way she was a deserter so I guess she dropped a couple of notches in his social group.

Lara squinted at me.

'How close was he?' he asked.

'He'd been up through the keyhole.'

Lara shook his head. He didn't like the idea of me being close to his tower.

'Who is General Castillo to give me orders?' Lara snorted.

'I kill the gringo then?'

'Sure,' Lara said. 'It will be good for the merchants.' Lara measured me with his eyes. 'He's got long legs. He might jump the wall.'

Pablo laughed. 'No he won't. My arm's rested.'

'What if I do?' I said.

'You won't,' Pablo said.

'I might. Then what?'

'I said I'd let the men go that made it over the wall.'

'Sure,' I said.

'You doubt my word?'

'Yeah,' I said to Pablo. 'What you gonna do? Kill me?'

Pablo laughed at that. 'It's too bad you don't have nine lives like a cat. I could kill you every couple of weeks.' He was trying to be friendly.

'If you're that sure, why not give me an unloaded gun, and stick some shells in my belt? I can't load on the run, and if I make it over the wall, it will keep your boys from following me too close.'

'It will slow you down,' Lara said. 'All that weight.'

'I'll chance it,' I said.

'*Muy bien,*' Lara called for a gun, a frontier Colt, the kind you load, bullet by bullet, into each empty chamber as you rotate the cylinder. It makes for slow loading. He filled my cartridge belt with .44-caliber shells. They were very sure of me. He even gave me my boot back.

And I knew I could make it. Pablo would let me get right up to the wall and jump for the top before he shot. Well, there was something he hadn't counted on.

I jogged a little and swung my arms, loosening up.

The sun was low now, in Pablo's eyes, but it also made me a great target silhouetted against it.

'You ready?' Lara asked.

'Sure,' I said, 'it's a good day for dying.'

Lara liked that. I think he must have been half Yaqui himself. 'Pablo?'

Pablo nodded. He laid his single-action uncocked pistol on the rough wooden table.

The general said, 'I will count to three.'

I nodded yes and when he said 'One' I lunged off to a running start. I was almost to the wall when Lara called out 'Three' and a step later I put my boot on the shoulder of the last man who had fallen atop another. I never touched the wall but dove over it headfirst. I guess I had about four feet of bodies and all the motivation in the world at my back. The shot came just as I cleared the wall and was a clean miss. I was over the wall with maybe a half an hour to sunset.

'Get that *cabrón*. I'll kill the man that doesn't find him.' Pablo was having one of his fits. I figured his order might confuse them and it did. Long enough for me to thumb three rounds into the Colt.

Then Lara's voice rang out and the shouting and rattling of guns stopped.

'Five hundred pesos in gold to the first man who finds him and another five hundred to whoever brings his head in.'

That did it. I took out for the brush like a jack rabbit looking for his nest. The trouble was I was a mighty big jack rabbit and the brush was scant. I had maybe ten minutes of light. If I could have blown out the sun, I would have done it.

I found a rabbit trail and was running good, but it was no use. I could hear the yips and horses' hoofs behind me and then a couple of shots as I stopped and turned. I was lucky to get a shot in the lead horse and drop him at almost a hundred yards. They had to rein in and the second horse went down over the first. I turned and ran again. A little thing like a dead horse or even a dead himself wouldn't stop one of Lara's soldiers. His own worthless life against enough money to make him rich. He could even be a land-owner and have his own *peones*. In what seemed like three cricket chirps they were closing in on me again.

'Hey, gringo. Big gringo. Over here.'

I whirled ready to shoot.'

'Jump off the trail and run this way.'

Why not? I jumped and ran, right through thorns and spiny branches, and fell straight down. I flailed out with my hands and a white figure broke my fall. 'Quiet,' he said. It was dark in that narrow deep dry wash but I could make out the face. It was the Indian I had helped make it over the wall a few years ago that same day.

'I see you come over the wall. I wait to see maybe I sneak back, cut you loose.'

'Name's Corcho Bliss,' I said. 'You want anything I got, just ask.'

'Name of Chimba,' he said. I found out later it meant a kind of duck. 'All even now. We run, yes?'

'Yes.' And run we did. The dry wash was straight-sided and deep enough to hide us. If they found our trail before dark, they'd still have to run us down on foot unless they knew where the wash went, and I figured we'd cut out from it and hide our tracks. After about fifteen minutes of loping along, I called a halt. I had been running after Chimba's white shirt but even that was getting difficult. I asked about pulling out of the wash and he said no. He knew a way he said that only he and a few others that lived around the hills knew. He walked on as sure of himself as a desert fox so I followed. The bottom was flat and sandy and not bad going.

After a couple of hours the moon came up and we went back into a trot.

Up ahead the wash split into two smaller ones. We took the right-hand one. It got so narrow I was almost running sideways. The moon was up high now and I could see the country around clearly, my head up above the rim of the wash now. Chimba slipped off into a rabbit trail running up the side of the wash and then trotted off down into a field of boulders.

My mouth was open and it hurt to breathe. I needed more air that I could get. I waved at Chimba, but he was already haunched down sucking at his hand. I dropped and dedicated myself to breathing. Then I heard a splash. Well I've seen a few mirages but I never heard one before. I looked up, breathing easier now, and Chimba was sucking his hand again, except it was cupped and had water in it. It's a good idea when you're dry and hot to drink water out of your hand. That way you can't drink enough to hurt you much.

My hand holds about a half a canteen though, and if it wasn't for my fingers leaking, I would founder just like a water-locoed horse.

'How long will it take them to find this place, Chimba?'

'Don't matter. We go now and they never find.'

'Hey, now!' He didn't even turn around. 'Okay, Chimba. You're the onliest game in town.'

He led the way up to the crest of a rock hill. As far as I could see it was rock, pink under the moon.

I took off my boots and tore a piece of my shirt off so as to tie them around my neck. He led off dogtrotting and following some kind of a trail I couldn't see. I hoped the Yaqui trackers couldn't either. When the moon went down we found a flat place and I went to sleep on that nice soft pink rock just like it was a feather bed in Mrs. Grandy's sporting house.

We were awake just before dawn. It was cold and I rubbed my arms and legs and skipped around a little.

'Where we at, Chimba?'

'Very close to Rio Largo.'

'What direction is the border?'

'What's a border?'

'Where's El Paso?'

'I don't know.'

'How far are we from Chihuahua?'

'What's Chihuahua?'

I gave up. He knew his country all right, but anything outside of that might as well have been on the moon.

'You figure on staying at the river?'

He nodded yes. 'Food there. Deer. I get you up close.'

I'll bet he would. Although I wasn't a bad hand at a stalk myself. Early that afternoon we saw the river. It was fast-moving, long and blue, and wound down towards the Pacific. I had a pebble under my tongue to ease my thirst, but the sight of that river made the pebble gritty in my mouth and I spit it out. It was dry when it hit the solid rock we were running on.

In a few minutes the rock started giving way to dirt and brush and in a bit we were running through pine trees. My feet had worn through my socks and I had ripped more of my shirt off to wrap around them. Even so they had formed blisters. The blisters broke and every step left blood on the rocks. I tried to put my boots back on, but my feet had puffed up like a pair of bloated cows.

Chimba just shrugged his shoulders. Maybe they would never get that far, but I didn't like the idea of leaving signs like that. No Indian, nor few Mexicans for that matter, would have feet the size of a full-grown grizzly. As I was thinking about it I heard the first baying of a dog, a hound. And then I could hear the pack and high above us, clattering down on the rock, came a group of riders. They weren't worried about crippling any horses on rock. Not when they could buy fifty first-class mustangs with five hundred pesos in gold.

Chimba looked as if he were going to swim for it until I called him back.

'They'll get us if we keep on running now. They'll work

both sides of the river, up and down, and soon more men will be coming. We need horses.'

'I agree with you. Wisdom like yours is a gift.'

'Thank you.' He wasn't quite as naïve as I thought. I knew when my leg was being pulled. 'They'll split up. Let's track down to the river, go upstream and then back here to wait for them to split up.'

He looked at my revolver. 'You shoot straight, White Eyes?'

'I shoot straight,' I said, 'Redskin.'

'Ayaha! I do it, Corcho.'

We ran into the water and my feet talked pretty to me until I started walking on the rock bottom. Then they stopped. When we trotted out to the hot sand, they cussed. Bad. In Spanish.

We came around, downwind, and made ourselves invisible in a clump of scrub oak and rabbit brush.

The dogs were singing, drunk on our close scent, running to it. When they hit the river, they ran in circles, barking angrily, nervous as to the men behind them. There were seven dogs in the pack.

The man in charge had boots on and a real all-leather saddle. The others sat on bare wood and wore huaraches.

'You, Juan and David. Take three dogs and go upstream. Benjamin, you and the others go down. Go one-half an hour. If you hear them, fire three shots. I will fire three and the others will hear and we will ride to meet you.'

'And if we hear no shots, Capitán?'

'Then, idiot, when the sun is there' – he pointed about a half an hour below the sun – 'you will cross the river and come back. They are very close, right, Cuevo?'

The Indian tracker nodded. He leashed three dogs and they started north. The others went south. And the captain loosened the cinch of his horse, let it drink a few swallows and then tied it in the shade, three steps from me.

He never heard me. I cracked him over the ear with my pistol barrel. I gave his pearl-handled pistol to Chimba. I said, 'Goddamn a man who won't carry a rifle. No knife either, the cute bastard.'

I waited about ten minutes, then signaled Chimba to fire three shots. He moved off to the left. I drifted to the right. We waited.

They walked right into our ambush. Chimba waited until I fired. My man fell and lay still. Chimba, smarter than I thought, shot a horse and then, using both hands to aim, shot the rider through the chest as he lay, a leg caught under his horse. The Indian tracker whirled and ran back out of sight. The dogs caught my scent and came running up. I shot all three in as many seconds. Then I was on the captain's horse, kicking it into a run. Even with my weight, the rested horse caught up with the runaway. I caught its bridle and saw a Winchester rifle in a saddle holster.

When I got back Chimba had a canteen filled and was munching on some jerky he must have taken from the dead horse's saddlebag. He had his revolver in a holster and a rifle in his hand. A bandolier was over one shoulder. The loops were full.

The other men came a-whooping, eager for the kill. They reined up when they saw the dead horse. 'Drop the guns,' I said.

From the other side, out of sight, Chimba called out, 'I shoot the fat one, eh, Corcho?'

'Drop the guns, boys,' I said. 'I've killed my man for breakfast, but I'm still hungry.'

There's no beating the drop. Not when you can't even see who's got it. They let loose of their rifles. Only one had a pistol and he pulled it out with his thumb and one finger. If they had had one chance in a hundred, it would have been a fight, but there wasn't. Even so, it was close. I had forgotten the little Yaqui tracker. It would have been all up with me if Chimba hadn't put a bullet an inch to my left. The Yaqui dropped his old single-shot Remington and caught himself on his arms as his leg folded in on him. Chimba was about to finish him off but I yelled 'No' and sent the Yaqui crawling over to join the group. I picked up a Winchester to throw it into the river.

'*Perdón, señor.*' The Yaqui was old for a wild Indian, more than fifty I would have guessed. He paid no more attention to his smashed leg than I would have to a sore finger. His Spanish, like most Indians', sounded like a toy piano. 'It is not in your mind to throw these magnificent arms into the river?'

'Yes,' I said, 'although these are not much as rifles go.'

Chimba said, 'He will not fight for a while. Maybe never.'

'He is yours,' I said, 'but I would like to let him have this rifle and a dozen cartridges. Maybe he could make it home.'

'But if he should meet with Lara?'

'That would be the last thing he would do.'

'My general would have me shot.' The little Yaqui grinned. Damned if he didn't seem to enjoy the debate.

'I guess we better move out.'

Chimba nodded. He stuck the Winchester in the saddle boot of one of the horses. He put the reins in the Yaqui's hands.

'My name is Juan Sánchez. They call me Chimba. I live in San Pablo del Borrego. When you heal, bring me my horse. I like venison,' he added as he turned away with his own horse.

He turned his horse west, up the river. I swung into the saddle of the captain's gelding, but I didn't follow. 'I'm going north, Chimba.'

'Then we go north, but my pueblo is to the west and we will be safe there.'

'Sure. Except I have to see – my wife.' I thought, 'Yes, sir, Corcho, your wife and Willy and maybe a chance to see Pablo just one more time.'

'I will go with you.'

'No, Chimba. Thanks. You and me, we are even. A life for a life and you got credit with me anytime you need it.'

He didn't get it right away, but when he did he gave me a big wide grin. 'Sure, Corcho. And if you need any lives saved, just send word to me, Chimba, in San Pablo del Borrego.'

'Corcho Bliss, El Paso, address known on this side of the river, your servant.'

We shook hands, Indian-style, just a touch of fingers and then an openhanded wave, and he trotted away, upriver.

Daytimes I spent in whatever shade I could find. After the sun dropped down to the top of the brush I'd saddle up and walk my stolen horse north, following whatever trails led in the general direction. The third day I figured I was close enough and then I was sure when that damn horse got his teeth on to the bit and we blasted our own trail right through the cactus. My better nature talked me into hauling that locoed horse's head away from the river after he'd put away a couple of swallows. I had to jump down and put my back into it just to swivel that ugly barrel head away from that watery mud. I guess he was a little tired of chewing cactus up for a mouthful of water. Still, I had cut out most of the spines before I fed or watered the brute.

I needed a horse so I tied him up to a snag in the riverbank and chewed some of that water myself. Then I picked out all the spines and burrs that I could get at and tried to figure out if I was up or down river from El Paso del Norte. If I was upriver, I could ride east and south, and if I was wrong, when I hit the ocean I could turn left and follow the river back up to Matamoros. Or I could go north and west and end up in Denver if I was wrong.

In times like that what you need is a scout's instinct. That and common sense. I decided to see what drifted down the river. I guess I expected to find a bottle with a message that said 'Downstream, Corcho.'

All I saw was three pieces of mesquite and a drowned prairie dog. I watered the horse again and thought about eating the prairie dog but I never liked them anyway and I couldn't bring myself to eat a drowned one. I could see white hunger wrinkles in my stomach, but many's the time I've gone hungry for three days and I had eaten the watery pulp of the cholla cactus along with a few skinned-out nopal strips, so I was not too weak, but I was hungry enough to eat a horse.

And I almost did. That brute behaved like every horse that has ever tried to bite me, kick me or throw me into a rattlesnake den. Before I knew what that brute was up to, he had worried the piece of wood out of the bank and into the river and when I caught sight of him, that sorry animal was trotting downstream along the river's edge. By the time I got to my feet he was around a bend. It was midday and I had stripped down to nothing to wash the dirt and burrs off. I grabbed my hat and revolver and took out after that horse. I had in mind a crippling shot so I could cut one piece out of him at a time. Meat won't spoil that way the way it will when you kill the whole animal.

I'm a good runner. The wet packed mud felt good to my blistered feet so I hit the turn in the river at full steam and ran smack bare-ass naked into the annual San Pablo-Bordensville barbecue. They had a big banner tied between a couple of flagpoles, one flying the Mexican red, white and green flag and the other the red, white and blue of the States. I tried to stop and run the other way but that mud kept me too long in the same place, and even as I was facing and trying to run away from all those women in sun-bonnets and straw hats, I went sliding backward into a mess of plates and kids. I grabbed a blanket as I skidded by and shook the plates loose. I had it around me and was up and running before anyone else moved. It was one of those friends-across-the-river barbecues or I guess I would have been shot right then and there. Nobody had a gun or didn't want to own up to a hideaway so I went flying right on through the picnic. I'll never know how I got a hunk of cake stuck on my gun barrel.

That crazy horse had his head stuck in a whirlpool and

was trying to back out but the driftwood had been sucked under and was snagged on something. I slipped his bridle off, got my teeth into his ear and climbed on. We went downriver at a run. I let the horse go until I couldn't hear any shouting behind me and then I started cracking him across the nose with my gun barrel until he stood still, then I tore a piece off that blanket long enough to halter him with. I knew where I was now. Downriver about ten miles from El Paso. With a locoed horse, a blanket and a pistol. I ate the piece of cake off my gun barrel while I thought it out. It was getting dark and I still hadn't come up with any ideas when I heard cows bawling and I got back in the brush quick. It's easy enough to lose steers crossing a river in the daytime. There is only one reason for doing it at night and as soon as the man riding point came along I could see I was right. He was mean-Texas with guns and knives all over him. He checked the river, up and down, built him a cigarette, and when the first steer came on up he squirted it into the water and the rest followed. He was lucky and he knew it. Some days those steers would have milled around all night long before they'd take it into their minds to rush into the water.

It wasn't deep. They never even had to swim for it. It must have been a natural ford. It took maybe a half an hour for about fifty steers and five cowboys to wade across and disappear into the black brush. I tied that horse to a bush but figured he'd be gone anyway when I got back. I walked upstream and swam across slow, without splashing, and with the .45 up out of the water.

I came down easy, staying in the shadow, and hunkered down to watch the trail leading up into the chaparral. I set my mind on a play I had been in and turned Indian for a while. The cowboy they left to watch for some angry Mexican ranchers couldn't wait. He lit a cigarette and I spotted him. I got scratched some, but I got behind him. He dropped his cigarette when my gun barrel touched his neck but he didn't say a word. I was quiet too.

'You like to go on living, cowboy?'

'Yes, sir.'

I would have been unnerved too.

'Don't turn around then. Drop your gun belt.'

He did.

When I told him to take off his pants, his breath whistled in, but I cocked the .45 for effect and he got out of his pants and shirt. He started on his boots but they were about three sizes too small.

'Let 'em be.'

His pants were high and tight but I left the buttons undone and let his belt out to the last notch. The shirt split down the back when I buttoned it. He had cotton drawers on, so he wasn't naked anyway.

'Where's your horse?'

'Up the trail about a rope's length.'

I took his gun belt with me.

His horse, an ornery-looking buckskin with a flop ear, eyed me and tried a halfhearted kick. I walked around him and unwound the reins from a mesquite branch. He turned but I got on all right and pulled his head up tight. He stood still then.

I called softly, 'There's a horse across the river. No bridle, but he's tied up next to a drifted log. See it over there white in the moonlight? Here's your rope. I'll leave your gun over by the log. I'll let your horse loose up around El Paso. If you don't talk much, I'll leave a few double eagles in the saddlebag. Okay?'

'Okay, mister,' he said, 'but I'll be goddamed if I don't go to herding sheep and let them Mexican mavericks find their own way across the river.'

I trotted back up the river and was well out of sight when I heard him hallooing for some help. I felt a whole lot better. Especially when I rode past where I had left my clothes and found nothing but some ashes where my clothes had been. Ashes and enough of my left boot to wear. I felt better with the half-burned boot on. The saddle was gone.

The Bip Dipper was upside down and turning east when I rode into Ciudad Juárez.

I had to stand on the saddle and look over the wall to see a light in Don Hilario's house. I called out and his study window on the patio opened up.

'*¿Quién es?*'

'It's Corcho, Don Hilario.'

The window slammed shut and then I could hear him trotting across the stone patio. I led the horse to the gate and waited. The gate swung open and Don Hilario gave me a big *abrazo.* I hung on to the reins with one hand and pounded him on the back with the other. It was like Don Hilario to say nothing about my clothes or my bloody half ear.

'I heard you were dead.'

'I heard the same rumor,' I said. 'Did Pearl make it back?'

'Do you mean Mrs. Bliss?' It was the first time I had ever heard Don Hilario snicker and it made me mad.

'What's so funny? I guess I can get married if I feel like it. I guess she's back and talking, if you know about it.'

'Back, yes. Not talking much. Willy asked for the money. He claimed Pearl as next of kin.'

'He would. And Pearl?'

Don Hilario smiled. 'She twisted some hair from the nape of his neck around her thumb and finger and marched him out. As she left, she said, "When Corcho shows up, tell him I'll be at the Lone Star Hotel." '

'I think I'll take another piece of hair out of Willy,' I said. 'So they're at the Lone Star Hotel.'

'She said *she* was at the Lone Star Hotel.'

'Do you think I can cross over with no problem?'

'I think so.' Don Hilario laughed. 'You have been killed again. There is a boy with the face of an angel and the tongue of the devil who says he met you with pistols in Mexico and left you dead.'

'Billy,' I said. He must not have been much of a bandit for he sure didn't last long with the 'Apaches'.

'Yes,' Don Hilario said. 'He refers to himself as Billy the Kid. He has a small group that he buys drinks for.'

'Where?' I said. 'Where?'

'He's in El Paso. Don't kill him there, son. Shoot him here. No one will mind. Another foreign gunman dead will mean nothing.'

'I owe him a favor that a dead friend wants me to pay. Anyway, I'm clean on this side and I'd like to stay that way.'

'All right. Money?'

'Have I got my twenty thousand dollars?'

'Yes.'

'Here?'

'No, but I can give you up to a thousand.'

'Five hundred will do.'

He called out then and a shotgun-toting Yaqui who watched over Don Hilario stepped out of the shadows. Don Hilario said something to him and he trotted off into the darkness.

'I like your choice,' Don Hilario said.

'If you mean Pearl,' I said, 'that was some choice.'

'I hope I live to see the offspring. They should be, ah . . . sturdy and most independent.'

'Don Hilario, if we ever have any, I will crate them up and send them to you. Maybe it will give you a start on your zoo.'

He laughed. He wanted a zoo for the city. The *alcalde* who ran the town was a rancher. When Don Hilario offered to house and feed the animals he was all for it until he found out that Don Hilario planned on beginning with coyotes, wolves and pumas. He got so mad that he offered to buy a special cage and put Don Hilario in it. The *alcalde* considered wolves and flies to have been two of God's biggest errors. When drunk, he would name others.

The Yaqui came up with a leather bag. It was wet in my hands. The drawstrings were tied but Don Hilario wouldn't let me untie them.

'Tell me how much it was,' he said and moved me away. There weren't many like him then and damn few now. He almost fooled me too. He was that smart. But I remembered just as I swung up in the saddle.

'Come on, Don Hilario. What bar does the kid hang out in?'

'A debt is a debt. It's your right. He often frequents a low place called The Last Candle. Good night.'

The Last Candle was a cabaret with dance-and-drink girls on the edge of the red-light district. I tied the horse just down from the sheriff's office. He was an old-timer and honest so I just tucked a hundred-dollar gold piece in the right saddlebag and left it there. Maybe that part-time rustler would get his horse back. A drunk wandered by me, and in a whisper that could have been heard across the river said, 'Hide the gun, old buddy.'

'Thanks,' I said. I'd forgotten how towns were on the Texas side. I left the belt and holster in the saddlebag and shoved the pistol in my left boot, my only boot, on the inside. Once I got into The Last Candle no one would be sober enough to notice except the bartender and he wouldn't be able to see below the bar.

I was wrong. A hard-eyed man almost as big as me tapped me on the shoulder. 'You can check the gun with me.'

'You guarantee no other loose hardware around?'

'Just mine.'

Before I could bend over he said, 'I'll get it.'

He reached down, flipped it out and put it back of the bar. He gave me a brass plate, number three.

I leaned on the bar and ordered whiskey and beer. I drank the beer, ordered another and took it over to the free-lunch counter. There wasn't much, but what there was I ate.

The bartender caught me by the shoulder and I slopped beer on my ripped stolen shirt. He was not as tall as me, but wide and heavy. He looked strong, but he had the wrong kind of eyes.

'This is not a charity organisation,' he said.

'I ordered a whiskey and two beers. Ain't that enough? Besides, your lunch is crumby. I got my hands dirty.'

I yanked his shirt to me and wiped my hands. When he bellowed and swung I kicked his feet out from under him. He hit the sawdust hard. I kicked sawdust in his eyes when he got to his knees, so he stayed there pawing at his eyes.

'Hold it.' It was the hard-eyed bouncer.

I did.

'You got any money?'

I took out a handful of gold eagles and showed him.

'Okay, mister.' He helped the bartender up by his hair. 'Tim, you are too dumb to talk. The man's got money. Serve him.' He turned to me. 'Sorry. Last week he refused to serve an Indian. So the Indian spends one thousand dollars across the river.' He sighed. 'Care for a job?'

'No, thanks,' I said, 'but I like a tolerant man. Buy you a drink.'

He looked around. 'Whitey.' An albino came over from a card table. He was a dealer. 'Watch the door.' The albino nodded and went back to the table.

'He's got a hide-out?'

'Yeah. Shoulder holster. All of my employees are licensed to carry guns. Sheriff Hollinger – '

'Bob Hollinger?'

'Yeah. That's him.' He took a long look at me. 'Do I maybe know you? I'm Jack Dooley.'

'Name's Floyd Wheatley,' I said. 'No. Can't say as I have had the pleasure. I know who you are and you can keep that gun for a souvenir if you've a mind to.'

He laughed. 'The drinks are on me, Floyd. Sit?'

He pulled a chair out from under a drunk and a swamper

came over and rolled him into a corner.

'When I worked cattle we treated them about like that but we tried not to bruise them.'

He laughed hard at that. 'You're right, Floyd. I get to thinking sometimes that there are only drunks and the ones about to get drunk.'

'You're looking at the latter,' I said. 'A hundred bucks if I could borrow a shirt and pants that fit. And maybe another boot. Or even two.' I looked over at that big bartender. 'He'll do!'

Dooley understood me.

I got up.

'Condition.' He held up a finger and I sat down again. 'You tell me how a man with a pocketful of gold eagles is dressed like a bum . . . and wearing one boot.'

I said yes and skipped behind the bar. The bartender argued but Jack told him to put on his street clothes and give me his good ones. The shirt fit fine and so did the boots. I offered him my old burned left boot but he didn't want it. The pants just reached the top of my new boots and they fit fine around the waist once I ran a piece of twine through and cinched it up about a foot.

'Okay,' Jack said. 'Shoot.'

'No names, but there's a blonde in town that has got the biggest boobies this side of New Orleans.'

His mouth opened wide. 'Willy's daughter!'

'No names.' I gave him my heroic no-smiling look.

'Right. Sorry, Floyd. I just didn't figure that Pearl . . . Oh. Sorry. Go ahead.'

'Whiskey,' I yelled. The bartender banged the bottle down on the table.

'Have a drink,' I said.

'Don't drink.'

'What's whiskey here?'

'This kind or the other?'

'What's the difference?'

'Two bits.'

'I don't mean the price, I mean the quality.'

'Ain't none. But if you're drinking with the boss, you pay two bits. Otherwise you pay four bits.'

'All right. Bartender, every time I drink one you add up another four bits for you. I am a temperance man myself and may God help Carry Nation in her noble work.'

'Amen,' Jack said. We clicked glasses and threw one down. It was not bad whiskey and I said so.

Jack shook his head. He said, 'Where have you been that my whiskey tastes good?'

I tried it again and it did taste good. 'South in Chihuahua. It sure beats that sotol I was stuck with.'

'Salud.'

We drank again. Funny how liquor will fire up a man. The Deacon, who was always a cold one, would hop the ugliest whore in Tombstone if he was drunk. He used to say that alcohol would pump up a dick faster than a manometer. I laughed, and when Jack asked me why, I told him.

'What's a manometer?'

'Takes your blood pressure. Ain't you never checked your blood pressure?'

'No,' Jack said, 'but when I get me a hole she spurts right out.'

That set me to laughing.

'Come on, Floyd,' he said, 'tell me about Pearl . . . I mean the blonde.'

'Oh,' I said. 'I guess she chased me over half of Chihuahua.'

'She chased you? Come on, Floyd.'

We drank up.

'You got any good ones here, Jack? I'm feeling horny.'

'With that blonde just three blocks away?'

Yeah. Lot of good that'd do me. Except I was married. Of course I was. And to Pearl. 'You're exactly right.' I started to get up and thought better about it. 'One more drink,' I said.

We had one.

'Hey, Floyd,' Jack remembered to ask, 'how did you get that outfit?'

'The bartender gave it to me.'

'Yeah. That's right. Well, *salud*.'

'*¡Salud!* Hey,' I said, recalling Don Hilario's words, 'is there a blue-eyed kid hanging out in here? Likes to talk a lot about gunfighters?'

'Yeah.' Jack stopped grinning. 'Friend of yours?'

'No. But I got some business with him. Can you tell him something?'

'Sure.'

'Just say . . . say that Floyd's back.' I was having trouble with my words and Jack wasn't hearing too well. 'Tell him that Floyd is going to cut his cute little throat some night and he'll wake up in hell facing the wrong way.'

'What's that?' Jack says.

'I don't know. I guess you're always looking where you been instead of where you're going. Like me. Looking back.' I was about to cry, but my pride wouldn't let me. Not even in front of an old friend like Jack. 'What the hell kind of a life is that?'

'Hell, I don't know,' Jack said. 'What you want me to tell that kid?'

'Tell him that friends of Corcho Bliss, the man he killed, have put up a thousand dollars for the man who'll ride across the river with the kid's head in a gunny sack.' I stood up and made it to the bar. 'That hundred make it?' I asked.

'Sure,' the bartender said. 'I'll get your change.'

'No,' I said. 'You keep it for me. If I don't come back or anyone calls for it, you keep it.'

'Yes, sir! Thank you, sir.'

I did it because I learned from the Deacon that a man will never give you away if he's going to lose by it. Only if he makes something. That bartender would never have heard of Floyd Wheatley. And he wouldn't talk about a man whose money he was holding. The law or maybe relatives might want it back.

The three blocks went fast and before I knew it I was in the hotel. I guess it was about three. There was a clerk sleeping in a chair. I looked through a book for a Miss Pearl Harper. I found Willy's name. But no Pearl. And there was only one name on the register. Then I saw Mrs. something and I went back and read very carefully. I found it. Mrs. Floyd Wheatley. It looked like a woman's handwriting.

Pearl, at least, figured we were married. I looked for the key and I couldn't quite focus on the numbers but I closed one eye and read the register. She was in 14. That was Pearl. I knew the hotel. The only bath was right next to her room. I went on upstairs.

The walls were pushing me from one side to another. 'I have been too long without a drink,' I thought. Maybe Willy would have one. He was across the hall in 7.

I leaned against his door. I knocked cnce and said, 'Willy?'

Then the hotel rocked and I fell back and hit Pearl's door and then I went all the way back and into as deep and safe a sleep as I can ever remember.

Sunlight and whispering woke me up. My eyes wouldn't open. The muscles were all tied in knots. I squinted them open. I lifted up on one elbow and tried to see past my feet. I was in a bed and it felt good and the whispering stopped and when I turned my head, very slowly because of pain, there was Pearl and Willy.

Pearl looked real good. She was wearing what I thought was a conservative dress for her, but when she bent over to slip another pillow under me, that little chain got caught between those pretty snowballs with cherries on top and I said, 'Get rid of Willy. I just remembered something I wanted to tell you.'

'You can tell me in front of Willy,' she said.

'Okay. Pull off your dress and climb into bed.'

I had already put a pillow over my head so she didn't hit me directly, but the jarring was playing hell with my eyeballs.

'Pearl,' I said, 'that clicking you hear is not billiard balls but my eyeballs a-rolling around in their sockets. Peace?'

She whacked me on the bottom of my feet and I went straight up.

'What's the matter, Corcho?' Pearl asked.

'Look at that foot,' Willy said. 'Did Lara turn you over to those Yaqui trackers?'

Willy was dressed even dandier than when I first met him. He could have been a Chicago banker or even a New Orleans pimp. He looked that elegant.

'No. I got to thinking that if the good Lord had intended us to wear boots he would have put leather on our feet. So I threw them away and then ran a day or so through some rock and prickly pears to toughen 'em up.'

Pearl touched my foot and I yelled.

'They ain't so tough yet,' I apologised. 'But give me a few more days and they'll be as good as any horse's hoof.'

'Oh, Corcho. What did they do to you?' Pearl had a soft look in her eyes. 'Corcho, your ear. That's dried blood.' She whimpered a little.

'Pablo got to like me. A fly was bothering me, and as I had my hands tied and couldn't swat it, Pablo just shot it off my ear.' I was feeling good. Sleep has always been the best medicine for me.

'Willy, why don't you get me a cold beer? And order me a couple of steaks with eggs.'

'The beer and steak are on their way, son.'

'Willy, you have all the finer feelings of a Laredo card sharp. We are on our honeymoon.' I pointed to the door.

'What do you mean by that, Corcho Bliss?' said Pearl, and she started tapping the floor with one foot.

'I just thought . . . maybe . . . you would like to . . . talk a little. Yeah, we could talk a little while Willy goes out for my steak.'

'Talk!' said Pearl. 'You were talking a little last night. Who, if your *legal* wife is not too impertinent, is Carmencita?'

'Carmencita. Yeah . . . Carmencita. Oh. That's the girl that Lara took away from Tex. That gent that Pablo shot down. As for the girl, well, I don't know if he had the time to, uh, marry her or not before he married you . . . that is, Lupita.'

'Did you help her, too?' Pearl snapped.

'Now hold on,' I said. 'I am gettting angry. I have suffered some pretty big outrageous slings and arrows of fortune.'

'Corcho.' Willy and Pearl looked at me as if I had two heads, and I might as well have had.

'Look,' I said, 'I have been running, riding, crawling, and naked in a picnic, and, well, I have had just a couple of hours of sleep since three days and – '

Something in Pearl's face stopped me.

'What's wrong?'

'You have been in this bed almost thirty hours,' Willy said. 'We do not mean to be difficult with you, son, but – '

'Goddamn it, Willy, do not call me "son". If you can't say Corcho – ' I crunched down on that name. I had gotten used to it and it could cost me my neck. 'Floyd,' I said. 'If you can't say Floyd, say political son, because that's what I am legally in Spanish.'

'Yes.' Willy was a smooth one. 'Son-in-law and *hijo político* are too long, so Floyd it will be, and a fine name indeed. A maker of chicken coops I believe is what the name means, an honorable if unrewarding profession, but all in all – '

'Willy, why don't you go away?' Then it hit me. 'I have been in this bed for two nights?'

'Yes,' Pearl said.

'How did you get my clothes off?' I asked Willy.

'We had trouble,' Willy said.

'We?'

Pearl was beet-red. 'After all, I am your legal wife even if you don't like it.'

'Who said I didn't like it? How do I know? I ain't tried it yet.'

'What do you mean?' Pearl was still snappish. 'And don't put on that simple cowboy act with me.'

'Pearl,' I said, 'I have an idea. Send Willy away and we'll talk about that marriage.'

There was a rap on the door and a boy came in with a tray. There was a half a steer and a pail of beer with a mug. I picked up the pail and drank it down about half. Then I turned to the steak and eggs and it wasn't nearly as big as I had thought.

'Sure, Corcho,' Pearl said, I'll talk to you after we get back.'

'Back?' I said between bites. 'Back from where?'

'We have to deliver the guns,' Willy said.

I stopped eating.

'Lara is up here with money?'

'Yes,' Willy said.

'He didn't send someone else?'

'No. The last man he sent up to buy guns, six months ago, is still looking for them.'

'Where'd he go for them?'

'Paris, that's in – '

'Yeah, I know,' I said. 'France. *Henry the Fifth.* I played a bastard.'

'Corcho!' Pearl said.

'It was a legitimate part and call me Floyd on this side of the river. That name could make a widow out of you.'

Pearl just nodded and began to whisper 'Floyd' to herself.

'Where's he buying guns in Paris?'

'The last Lara heard he was looking for automatic weapons in the house of a certain Madam Fifi.'

'Fifi's, huh?'

'*Oui,*' Willy said.

'What did Lara say?'

'He called him, among other things, a bandit.'

I laughed. I could imagine the other things Lara had said.

'He's got ten times that in the tower.'

'Tower?' Willy said. 'Tower?'

'The Texan told me. The one Pablo shot. Remember?'

'The general that Lara pulled off that train to shoot mentioned the tower, too,' Pearl said. 'I heard him.'

'Yeah. I thought it was opium smoke until Pablo shot Tex. Tex told me that the loot was worth more than a million dollars. I got a map to it,' I added.

'Son!' Willy said in his affectionate voice.

'Willy,' I warned him with a fist, 'I'll bounce you off that wall.'

'Floyd, as soon as we can arrange our affairs, I suggest that we recover all of that stolen treasure and return it to its rightful owners if, of course, they are not dead or otherwise non-locatable.'

'Of course,' Pearl said, 'you might put an ad in the Bombay *News* or the Moscow *Herald*.'

'Well' – Willy shrugged – 'if we can't find the rightful owners . . .'

'And if you did stumble over a rightful owner?' Pearl twitched her nose at Willy.

'Why, Pearl! I would, of course, return the property minus a minimal fee for my time and trouble.'

'Hold on.' I had finished the steak, eggs and beer. 'What time and trouble are you referring to Willy?'

'Ours, Floyd, my boy. Ours. With the money from the sale of the arms, we will enlist an elite group of capable men and we will rescue that treasure and bring it safely back.'

'And if we did find the treasure and Lara didn't bury us with it, what would be my share?'

'Why it will be substantial, Floyd, substantial, and I will call any man a liar who says differently!'

'Willy, I got a substantial map. It will show me where the cave is. You are as smart as a tame coyote and you might find it. Nothing will get me anywhere near Lara. No matter what. And the tower is right smack in the middle of Lara land. So, you want to go, you give me a substantial share – in advance.'

'Floyd!' Willy loosened his tie. He fell back into a chair. 'Pearl, can this be my dear son-in-law, your husband? Is this the man we risked our lives for? Is this an old man's repayment? What has happened to the generous, humane, understanding man you chose for your life companion?'

'He's getting smarter,' Pearl said.

'Pearl!'

'No, Willy. You heard him. I wouldn't go back for any amount of money.'

'But, Pearl' – Willy was almost crying – 'there could be millions of dollars of loot there. Diamonds, emeralds, gold. A king's ransom.'

'That's right,' I said. 'I'll sell my share for fifty thousand dollars in gold.'

Willy jumped to his feet. He took his hand away from his heart. 'On the other hand, as you pointed out, it may be a fable. A myth. There might not be a thing there.'

'That's right. Make me an offer.'

'Let me see the map,' Willy said.

'Get me a pencil and paper.'

'What?' Willy screamed. 'You are going to draw a map and then try to sell it to me for fifty thousand dollars?'

'The other one got washed away along with my right boot,' I said. 'But I memorised it.'

Willy shook his head just like a steer that's been tailed so as to take the fight out of him. But he pulled out a small gold pencil and a white envelope.

I sketched in everything except the last turn and the keyhole to the cave and stopped.

'Go on.' Willy was breathing on my neck. He thumped me on the head. 'Finish it. Finish it.'

'Make us an offer,' Pearl said. 'Then he'll finish it.'

'Well,' Willy said, 'how about one thousand dollars and a share?'

'No,' I said.

'Well, that's my last offer,' Willy said.

'Mrs. Wheatley,' I said to Pearl, 'will you take care of this matter?'

'No,' Willy said. 'No agents.' Willy pulled at his nose and said, 'two thousand dollars.'

'You got the gold on you, Willy?'

'Yes,' he said.
'It's a deal.'
'It is?' Willy hit himself in the head. 'You just want the two thousand?'
'The money, Willy.'
'Yes. Of course. You finish the map.'
I did while Willy got his money belt off. He counted out the money.
'You keep the money for us, Pearl,' I said.
'Corcho!' Pearl squealed. 'You do trust me.' She was all smiles.
'More than Willy,' I said. 'And Floyd, Floyd, Floyd is my name.'
'As soon as we deliver the guns, Floyd' – Willy never forgot – 'we shall organise our expedition and you shall receive a share. No, no.' He stopped my yell. 'I insist. It is only fair. You deserve a share, and as my partner and son-in-law, I trust you.'
'Pearl,' I said, 'how do you feel about honeymoons?'
'They are for people who fall in love, get married in a church and – '
'You want to try it again in a real church?'
The second I said that I wondered what had come over me. I guess I was getting old. 'On second thought, Pearl,' I said, 'I am just a beat-up ex-bandit who – '
She was on me by then and I couldn't say another word. Pearl squirmed a little and said, 'Do you mean it?'
I meant to say no, but the way she squirmed and stuck her tongue in my mouth addled me and I said, 'Yes.'
It got awful hot in that room and before I knew it Pearl was about half out of her dress and I heard Willy say, 'Um, yes . . . well . . . I'll see you children later.' I heard the door slam and then Pearl's breast popped right up out of that dress and I had never seen anything so perfect in my life. But by then she was yanking and pulling and all of a sudden her clothes were all off and she was that same marble color all over and I thought what a goddamn fool I had been. Pearl made love just like she did everything else. No half-

way about her. When we finally made it, I could only think of a bucking mare that was about to throw me, so I grabbed on and made the best ride I could.

'Honey' – Pearl cuddled up to me – 'that was the nicest honeymoon I ever had.'

'Short, though! Hey,' I yelled. 'What do you mean the nicest one? How many you had?'

'Just two. You never asked, but I'm a widow.'

'A widow?'

'Yes,' she said. 'I'll tell you about it.'

'Not now,' I said. 'Later.' This time I made a better ride but I got scratched up some and bit a little. After a while I held her off and said, 'Whoa, girl. Hold on. I have a weak heart.'

'That's not what's weak.' Pearl grinned.

'Pearl,' I said, 'I don't want to know a thing about your first husband except how long did he last.'

'Just one week,' Pearl said.

'Yeah, that figures.'

Pearl got a charge out of that and she got to tickling me. Well, I've never had much to do with regular girls. I mean the kind you don't pay off. The good girls I always paid first and the nice ones you left the money on a table when you left the room. She had me going and I got to hoo-hawing and then Pearl got to giggling and I guess that's why we didn't hear the tap on the door.

The door swung open and I saw the hotel clerk with his hand in the air. His eyes were bigger than his mouth and he had a big mouth.

'Shut that door!' I yelled.

Pearl screamed and dove under the covers. The clerk grabbed the doorknob and backed out slowly. He held it open a bit and said, 'The sheriff will be here in a couple of minutes.'

I grabbed a gold ten-dollar piece and stuck my hand through the door. 'I'm the lady's husband. I got in late last night. This should pay the extra charge.'

'That is not the way we do things at the Lone Star Hotel, Mr. Wheatley.' He was a sneaky little bastard.

'Then I'll kill you, you goddamn sex maniac,' I said. 'Spying on a man and his wife and them both naked. Get that sheriff over here quick. And if you've got a wife or a mother, I'll be talking to her, too.'

'No, sir. No offense. My mistake, sir. I'll just sign you in myself, sir.' He clicked the door shut and trotted down the hall.

'What did you do to be so afraid of the law officers?' Pearl asked.

'I killed a girl,' I said.

'Why?' Pearl asked.

'For being nosy,' I said.

Pearl started for me, but just then there was a rap on the door and both of us got to it and held it shut.

'Floyd.' It was Willy. 'We have a rendezvous in just two hours with our military people. The merchandise left an hour ago. I think we had better discuss the method of transfer.'

'What does he mean?' Pearl asked.

'How we get the machine guns to Lara and get the money to us,' I explained. And I wondered what Willy had in mind, for I had plans for Pablo. Lara I might shoot, maybe yes, maybe no, but Pablo was dead. He just didn't know it yet.

I went over with the first machine gun. Pablo was there, waiting. He kept those long skinny fingers away from his iron so I did the same.

'Goddamn gringo!'

'And a good morning to you,' I said.

'Hello, *amigo*.' Lara beamed. 'You pile those machine guns over there and we send you the money – good U.S. money. Gold!'

'Sure,' I said. 'We pile one machine gun up here on this bank, then you pile some gold in this boat. Then we go back and get another gun.'

'You don't trust me!' Lara looked black. 'After I got you married to that pretty gringa. I am ashamed to call you friend.'

'You certainly ought to be,' I said. 'How's Lupita?'

'Mean and loud,' Lara said. 'How's the gringa?'

'Like Lupita,' I said.

Lara laughed. 'Come on, Corcho, show me how this gun shoots and maybe I'll give you some gold, eh?'

I fed a belt in and slammed a round in the chamber. 'Throw something that floats into the river,' I said, looking at Pablo's hat.

'No, you goddamn *hijo*, you,' Pablo spluttered. He was too mad to cuss in Spanish or English.

I reached out and plucked it off his head and threw it in the river. He yanked his gun out but Lara had put his big hand over the muzzle. 'Work now, Pablo. Play later,'

'Yes, my general.' Pablo spit at my boots. 'Later we play a little. Me and this *cabrón*. We play all right.'

I let the hat move down about three hundred yards and then aimed low, like Willy explained, and let the bullets walk up to the hat. I fired short bursts and on the last one Pablo's mushroom hat changed into a small flurry of snow.

The men cheered. They liked shooting. Especially when they had the triggers. Even Pablo said 'Goddamn!' without adding gringo.

Lara said, 'You teach my men how to use this?'

'Sure,' I said. 'Part of the service. Who's first?'

'*Yo*,' Pablo said.

I showed him once more, slow, how to load and fire short bursts so as not to warp the barrel or get it so hot it would heat-fire automatically. Then I showed him how to traverse. Pablo had a feeling for guns. He loaded and fired without a hitch.

Pablo grinned. Without his jungle hat and with his teeth white against his face he looked almost human. But as far as I was concerned he was a dead man.

We ferried over the guns. Pablo would fire a few bursts and then Lara would send the gold over. This went on until there was just the one gun left.

I got in the boat with the gold coin for the next-to-last machine gun.

'Where you goddamn go?' Pablo asked.

'*Sí*, Corcho. Where and why?' asked Lara.

'Once you get that last machine gun I don't think you will send me back. Not alive anyway.'

'Corcho!' Lara said '*¡Concuño!* You wound me!'

'*Concuño*.' When two or more unfortunate Mexicans marry sisters they have a new relationship. All the men become *concuños*. I guess that Lupita and Pearl were still mixed up enough in his mind that he decided we were at least *concuños*.

'I'm going back. I'll send the gun over and you send the gold back.' Lara coughed at that and Pablo snickered. He had a great sense of humor that day.

'Corcho, we are short of gold. So we trade you for the last machine gun.' Lara ducked behind a soldier as he spoke and held him as a shield. 'You got a dozen rifles pointed at you, *concuño*, so don't draw.' I didn't and Pablo picked out my pistol.

'You think Willy's dumb enough to send a machine gun over here for me?'

'You're his son-in-law,' Lara said. Mexican families are like that. You sell the family cow to help a sick third cousin who lives a hundred miles away.

'Willy won't do it,' I said.

'Yes he will,' Lara said.

'Maybe we send him an ear to convince him,' Pablo said.

'Hold on,' I said. 'You've just about used up my ears. Let me write Willy and tell him to send the gun and I'll give him a note to my bank for the $3,333.'

'That's good,' Lara said.

'We could send an ear for luck,' Pablo said.

'Not yet. Write the note. In Spanish.'

I did. Then we had to wait until Pablo found someone who could read it.

'You can have my money, Willy. Just give this note to Don Hilario and he will give it to you. Send the last machine gun over, and if Lara doesn't pay you for it, you can take it out of my salary. Don't send the machine gun if you don't see me upriver all alone. When you see me, send the gun over.'

I signed the note and one of Lara's soldiers went over in the boat. Pablo took me upstream. About five hundred yards.

'Pablo,' I said, 'when I hear you fire a burst from the machine gun, I swim the river. You keep your boys off the triggers until I make it over. Okay?'

'Okay goddamn.'

He grinned at me. I think Pablo really liked the men he killed. He felt good when he was able to shoot a man and I knew he meant to cut me down with that machine gun. He had been cutting driftwood in pieces at five hundred yards all morning.

The river was slow but deep where I stood. Pablo was dumb in some ways. He was the kind of a stupid man who is too stupid to know another man is smarter. He thought I might try to swim the river when he walked away.

'Look, gringo.'

All eleven machine guns were lined up and pointing at me. Even with those wild men behind the guns they couldn't miss and I knew it.

'*Muy bien,* Pablo. I won't move until I hear you fire and don't shoot near me.'

'Okay.' Pablo trotted off.

'See you in hell,' I called.

'Sure. In hell,' he called back.

Willy had the boat on its way back as soon as he saw Pablo walk away. I started breathing slow and deep, pushing oxygen into my blood.

Once I met a genuine Hindu fakir from Green River, Wyoming, who taught me how to hold my breath for more than three minutes. If you breathe deep and squeeze the air from your chest all through your body with each breath and keep it up for ten minutes or so, you can hold your breath two, three minutes. Of course you need ten minutes in between.

The boat reached the bank and Pablo waded out to heave it in. He carried the gun over to a flat, dry mudbank to one side of the guns. Then he called out something and the machine gunners stepped away from their guns. Pablo fed a belt into the gun and then yelled, 'Corcho, you *cabrón,* say hello to the devil.' Then there was a big puff of smoke and right after it the shock of the explosion.

I ran and hit the water and went deep. The current helped me but I kicked and pulled and kept on the bottom until my lungs burned and even then I bit my lip and counted to twenty before I came up. It was all I could do to breathe. The first thing I saw was splashes from machine-gun bullets. One of the brighter boys fired a burst that hit close so I went under again, heading downstream and for the far side.

I was maybe a mile down shore and a couple of hundred yards from the American bank when I came up again. There were no more shots. There were some fifty U.S. cavalrymen on the American side. They had a small howitzer and its barrel was smoking. A trooper rode out and let me hang on to his stirrup as soon as I could stand. He walked his horse back while I pushed air in and out of my aching lungs.

Up on the bank I waved to their officer, a lieutenant. 'Thanks,' I said. 'I owe you one.'

'Not at all. You were on our side of the river. I had you triangulated.'

'That's what I thought they were trying to do,' I said.

'A triangulation is a geometric exercise.'

I whistled. 'Now ain't that something. I get my ass saved by geometry and a howitzer. Where is my partner, Willy Harper?'

'With the sheriff. I believe he is under arrest.'

'What for?'

'What for? What effrontery! You have been gunrunning, selling defective equipment and provoking a friendly power. What for!'

'Look,' I said, 'we sold some firearms to a friendly power. Willy's got a license. And I think they did the provoking and that equipment was not defective. Well, I do think that last gun was defective, but if you'll look on the bill of sale, it was guaranteed defective.'

'Guaranteed defective! Guaranteed defective!'

'Do you always say things twice?' I asked.

'Do I always say things twice? Do I always – Arrest that man and bring him along!'

The lieutenant rode off. He had red hair and green eyes and that's a bad combination. Makes for an angry man. There were some more officers and some civilians and Pearl. I shrugged at her and she came running over and hugged me. I felt funny, her hugging me in front of all those men.

'Pearl,' I whispered, 'wait until tonight. We can't sport around in front of all these officers and ladies.'

She drew back her fist. When I covered up, she kicked me in the shin.

'You mean to say that I'm not a lady?'

'Yes, Pearl, I mean no . . . You are a lady and I'll bet you are also the best rough-and-tumble fighter that ever wore blue garters.'

'Corcho Bliss,' she yelled, 'you are impossible!'

I hissed at her and she turned white. She covered her mouth with one hand while tears filled her big blue eyes. I hugged her and told her to hush, that she could call me Floyd and everything would be all right. But it wasn't.

Sheriff Bob Hollinger was there and he turned very slowly and looked straight at me. He had pulled a gun when he heard my name.

'Corcho. It's you all right. Corcho Bliss. You are supposed to be dead.'

Bob had a tight look around his eyes. He was in his seventies, but you wouldn't make a play against him unless you had no other choice.

'My name is Floyd,' I said. 'Floyd Wheatley. I been working in Mexico and I'm in a hurry to get back.'

'No,' Bob said. 'No, I got a warrant for you. If you're Corcho Bliss.' He whirled on Pearl. 'What's his name?'

'Husband,' Pearl said. 'He's my bliss. I mean Mr. Floyd. Mr. Floyd, uh . . . Wheatley.'

Willy stepped forward. He said, 'I got your note and have deducted $3,333 for the machine gun and three dollars for the dynamite.'

'Dynamite?' the sheriff asked. He was pulling on his long, droopy white mustache and he was sure enough putting a few things together. 'Was there dynamite in the barrel of that new-fangled repeating repeater?'

'Why, Floyd. I think the sheriff has something there. That would certainly make the type of explosion we saw across the river. What carelessness!'

Pearl tucked her arm in mine. 'If you don't mind, Sheriff' – she peered over her nose at him, speaking in her Eastern accent – 'we, my husband and I, are on our honeymoon and we would like to be on our way.'

'I shook Bob's hand. His left hand. He just let me pump away. 'Nice meeting you, sir. Yes, sir.'

'That's Corcho Bliss all right. Gene said so and he knew him.' Good old Billy. The nasty little sneak was over with the lieutenant. He must have remembered Gene calling me Corcho and probably looked my name up in one of his two-cent books. 'I put in a claim for the reward right now,' Billy said. 'I identify him. The reward's mine. Right, Lieutenant?'

'No, Lieutenant,' I said. 'Bob knew me the moment he set eyes on me. I surrender to you, Bob.'

Billy's eyes squinted. Tears came. He screeched at me, 'You goddamn son of a bitch. You'd try to fuck me out of my reward. Well, you can't, you son-of – '

The lieutenant's green eyes and mouth were as green as they would ever get and his face was as red as his hair. He held an Army .45 in his hand. And he had laid Billy out cold.

'Filthy beast.' He bowed to Pearl and then to the other women. 'My apologies, ladies.'

'Put him in a cell,' Bob said. His young skinny deputy put his hand on my arm.

'No!' Bob roared. 'The other one. There on the ground.'

'Okay, Bob, but what for?'

'Disturbing the peace,' Bob said. 'Then fine him whatever he's got and book him for vagrancy.'

'You don't much look like Corcho,' Bob told me. He was a single hell-raiser that always carried a gun.'

'I'm married,' I said.

'Yes,' Bob said, as if he hadn't heard. 'You couldn't be Corcho Bliss, not married to a nice girl like that.'

'In that case,' Willy said, 'let's be off. We have many things to do. Thank you, Lieutenant, for your aid, unnecessary as it turned out.'

'Unnecessary! Unnecessary!'

I laughed out loud.

The lieutenant turned to a little man with a hard collar and a tie under a derby hat. In between was a soft white face. He had one of those half mustaches that you see on dudes. But he had the eyes. I could tell.

'Pinkerton,' I whispered to myself.

'Pinkerton Detective Agency, James Bell.' He pointed at me. 'That man is Corcho Bliss. He's got a train-robber charge waiting for him in Denver.'

'Naw,' Bob said. 'You're wrong. He ain't Corcho.'

Bob was all right. He was never the kind of a sheriff that would throw a man in jail just for the hell of it unless he figured the man was bad for his city. Then he'd throw down on the devil himself.

'Go home, little man,' Pearl said.

The Pinkerton man waved a handbill in front of Bob's face. The lieutenant saw it too.

'He's right, Sheriff.'

'Well, I'll be dogged,' Bob said. 'You sure fooled me.'

'Lieutenant,' the Pinkerton said, 'that man is very dangerous. Could you put a squad of soldiers on the jail until I get a Denver law officer here? It'll just be a day or so.'

'Lieutenant,' Pearl said, 'no. Not my husband!'

'Sorry, ma'am,' the lieutenant said. 'He'll be in no longer than a day if he isn't this outlaw Bliss.'

When Bob turned the key in my cell lock, the Pinkerton man slipped out his post-office art again. 'You don't recognise this man, Sheriff?'

'Them post-office pictures ain't much.'

'You mean it's not a good likeness of Corcho Bliss?'

'Well, that was made more'n twenty years ago. I heard he had his head blowed off.'

'Killed!' The Pinkerton man cocked his head at me. 'He looks alive to me.'

'That gent' – Bob sucked at his hollow tooth – 'looks alive all right. You aim to prove he's Corcho Bliss?'

'Mister?' Billy was sitting on his bunk. 'You get me that reward if I prove he's that there Corcho Bliss?'

'Sure thing,' the Pinkerton man said.

'In writing,' Billy said.

'In writing? Well now, that is different. In writing I'll have to reduce my offer. After all, I caught him and brought him in.'

Quick as a rattler Billy was shaking his cell door. A freckle-faced, blue-eyed mamma's boy who, in spite of all that, would have been kicked out of a scalp hunter's camp. Maybe that's what happened with the 'Apache' gang.

'I called him out for you. I know him.'

'Where did you know him from?' Bob asked.

'Mexico.'

'What year, son?' Bob was talking to him like you would a nervous horse.

'Last April.'

'1911?'

'Yeah, 1911.'

Bob shook his head at the Pinkerton man.

'Young man – ' The Pinkerton man removed his derby and fanned his face. He had a habit of holding his lips up tight till his mouth looked like the ass end of a plucked chicken. 'Young man, did you know Corcho Bliss when he was engaged in skulduggery?'

'Sure. He was doing plenty of it.'

'What?' I asked.

'That,' Billy said. 'What he said.'

'Where?' I asked.

'In Mexico. I saw you.'

'In Mexico,' Bob said. He shrugged again. 'We sure ain't in Mexico.'

'How can you identify him?' The derby was working faster now and I moved over a little just to catch the breeze, but he jumped back.

'Well, all you have to do is – ' Billy stopped. 'I want half.'

'Half of what?' the Pinkerton man said.

'Half of that there reward! That's what.'

'You want five hundred dollars?' He showed us the circular then. It was me all right. Drawn from an old daguerreotype and printed on cheap paper. It said 'Harold Bliss, known as Corcho Bliss' under the drawing. Then in big letters it said 'Reward. $1,000 for information leading to his arrest. Wanted for train robbery and murder.' In those days the first charge was the most serious.

'Is that all?' Billy sneered. 'You wasn't so much, was you?' He nodded his head. 'Put it into writing and I'll tell you how. I guess' – his voice took on a strut like Texas Jack in the *Scout's Revenge* – 'I guess I'm the only man in the world now that my dear friend and saddle pal Gene Little . . . ' He looked around. The Pinkerton man kept on fanning himself. Bob was in a chair now loading a pipe. I began to whistle softly.

I'll swear he almost cried. His eyes looked wet and he stopped for a minute. I wondered what had ever made Gene take up with him. I wondered if I had been a little like Billy. I hoped not.

'Anyway,' Billy said, 'I can tell you how to find him out. I mean get him and his name certified.'

'Hurrah!' I said. 'I always wanted to be certified.'

'Shut up.' The Pinkerton man was all business.

He took out a pad and borrowed Bob's offered pen. The kid kept grinning at me. The Pinkerton man passed the note on to Billy. He read it, moving his lips slowly to follow the words.

'Want me to read it to you, kid?' I said.

'Piss on you, Corcho.' He handed it back. 'You sign it, Bob,' he said.

'Go to hell,' Bob said.

'You son of a bitch! You sign that or I'll tell everyone you're a-helping Corcho Bliss and – '

Just then he got a pot of cold coffee in his face. Bob sat back down and got his pipe going.

'Ask the sheriff, whose name is Mr. Hollinger, if he would please witness this document,' the Pinkerton man said. They were good. I never met one I liked, but it was a natural prejudice I guess and I never claimed they weren't first-rate detectives.

'Please sign that promise, Mr. Hollinger.' Billy kept his eyes on the floor.

'Why sure, son. It's part of the job.' He said that last part to me.

Bob signed the document just as the door began to sound like one of those little Army drums. I groaned. It had to be Pearl and I had myself enough trouble at the moment.

There were some high-pitched yells and I caught some words about 'false arrest and justice' and then the door flew open and Pearl marched in with Don Hilario and the deputy.

'Sheriff Hollinger! I have a lawyer here and you let Floyd go and stop beating him and I'll sue everyone and if that isn't enough, I'll hire a newspaper and then – '

'Hold on,' Bob said. 'First, I promise to stop beating the prisoner. About letting him go . . . well, we're talking on it.'

'Please, Pearl,' I asked, 'just sit at the desk and try not to talk for a minute. Please, honey.'

'Why, Cor . . . Floyd,' she said. 'Honey!'

She went and sat right down. Left me with my mouth wide open. I decided right then that I would sweet-talk her more, that is if I ever got the chance.

'All right,' the Pinkerton man said, 'where's your proof?'

'He was an actor. He told us. Me and Gene. He was in Chicago and they called the play – ' The kid was so pleased with himself that he laughed out loud.

'Go on,' the Pinkerton man said.

Billy's mouth opened and closed just like a fresh-caught catfish. He finally got some words out.

'That's it. You just get the other people or actors or the boss of the show and they'll tell you who he is.'

'Did he say what name he used?' the Pinkerton man asked.

'Yeah, he said he was Floyd – ' He stopped.

'That's right,' I said. 'I told them I was in the theater and I was. Floyd Wheatley. It's my name.' I saw my lawyer, old Don Hilario, make a closed-mouth sign so I stopped. He knew more about people than I ever will. He even knew more than Willy, wherever he was, so I shut up.

The Pinkerton had his back to Billy. He was studying Pearl.

'Mrs. Bliss,' he said, 'when did you meet your husband?'

Don Hilario stepped forward. 'Mrs. Wheatley met *her* husband, Mr. Wheatley, through her father, William Harrison Harper, a well-known businessman.'

'He's wanted for murder, Mrs. Bliss,' the Pinkerton man said, 'but we could make a deal.'

'Slander is a serious offense, and under U.S. civil law, settlements can be extremely generous. Whom did Mr. William Harper murder?' Don Hilario did not even wrinkle his eyes. Oh, he was good.

'Sir, I was referring to the alleged murderer and train robber, Corcho Bliss, whose identity we shall presently prove.' The Pinkerton was no slouch either.

'In any case, a wife cannot testify against her husband,'

Don Hilario said. He offered his arm to Pearl. She almost took it and that would have been that.

She hesitated and the Pinkerton man said, 'But her lawyer says that she is not married to Corcho Bliss, and in court, if she so states, I shall either jail her for perjury or for being an accomplice of a murderer.'

That stopped Pearl. Then her chin went out and her eyes chilled. I yelled 'Look out' but I was too late. She let him have a pointed toe in the shin, and when he bent over, she crossed with her left and almost floored him. She was ready with a right but Don Hilario pulled her away.

The Pinkerton man took a few deep breaths. Then he said quietly, 'Corcho, I'll find someone. I'll put ads in a Chicago paper and I'll get someone who will remember. It may take time, but if you make me, I'll take the time, and then, I promise you, she'll go to jail, too.'

Never get too fond of horses, dogs or women. They can do anyone in. Even a low-down criminal like me.

'You just pulled my cork,' I said. Don Hilario smiled and Bob snorted. Billy knew that cork and Corcho meant the same, so he smiled. He was already spending five hundred dollars to celebrate my hanging.

'No!' Pearl yelled, and made a grab for Bob's gun. She almost got it but I yelled to warn him and he automatically covered his gun with his big delicate hand.

'All right, Pinkerton,' I said, 'you keep her out of it, and I'm the man on that poster.'

'Done,' he said.

'I'm Corcho Bliss. You write it and I'll sign it.'

'No, Corcho,' Pinkerton said. 'I don't need any paper from you. Do you want anything in writing?'

I just shook my head.

'Why not?' Billy screeched. 'Get it in writing,' he yelled at the Pinkerton man. 'Why don't you get it in writing?'

'I guess we're just different generations, eh, Pinkerton?'

He nodded.

'Just for kicks, how much do the posters total up to?' I asked.

'Posters?' Billy said. 'Posters? There's more'n one?'

'There are three rewards,' Pinkerton said. 'This little one for a thousand dollars is from the state of Colorado. There is one from the railroad for three thousand and then, of course, there is the big one from the Railroad Protective Association for five thousand.'

'You cheat. You dirty cheat. You no-good son of – ' Bob stuck a billy under his nose and Billy stopped. But he was so mad he banged his head on the bars.

'You waive extradition?' Pinkerton asked.

'Yes.' Maybe I could make a break on the transfer. I'd done it once before. All I needed was a few minutes alone with that dumb deputy.

'I will accompany you,' the Pinkerton said.

My hopes hit bottom. The Pinkerton was a very efficient little man.

Pearl stopped crying. She was too quiet. I didn't like her look at all.

'Pearl, you go back to the hotel now. Don't get near this jail until the sheriff tells you it's visiting time.'

She smiled, put her face up to the bars for a kiss and left still smiling.

'Pearl,' I yelled, 'don't you even think about – Pearl, there's a squad of soldiers around this jail!'

'The old boy taking over where you left off?' Billy asked.

'Here,' I said, 'dry your eyes.' I handed him my handkerchief. That set him off again until the sheriff reached for the coffeepot. Then he lay face down on his bunk.

The Pinkerton shook hands with me. When he told the sheriff that he would be around, Billy, face down still, asked, 'When you gonna give me the five hundred?'

'When he is convicted, the Pinkerton Agency will pay you. We have a special man in charge of paying people like you. He is a former child molester.' He tapped his hat on and left.

'I'm going to miss you, Corcho,' Bob said. 'Never knew who was the fastest, you or the Deacon.'

Billy snorted. 'Gene would have beat him easy.'

'It wasn't that,' I said. 'I was as fast as the Deacon, maybe a bit faster, but he was steadier. He just didn't give a damn and I always wanted to live.'

Bob nodded. 'I've been there,' he said. 'But folks know if I say I'll shoot, I'll shoot. Discourages amateurs.'

'I think maybe we would have killed each other,' I said, 'if I didn't try to pull too fast. Then he may have had time in between shots.'

'What the hell you mean, in between shots?' Billy was sitting on his bunk now.

'I'd like to show you,' I said, 'but I don't mind telling you that many's the snotty kid – '

Bob nodded. 'Many,' he added.

' – that,' I went on, 'has yanked a gun and fanned off five – '

'Probably six,' Bob said.

'You're right. Every cylinder loaded, and if he was lucky, he didn't shoot himself in the balls before he got his gun out.'

'And if he did,' Bob said, 'he might get six off.'

'Sure,' Billy said. 'I can do it myself against most of these clodhoppers.'

'Billy,' I said, 'I have seen a young man, your age, pull out a gun and empty it' – Billy nodded agreement – 'before a clodhopper eased his gun out, thumbed the hammer back and drew a bead on the fast-draw artist.'

'Yeah?' Billy was interested.

'The plowboy shot him dead with his only shot. Then he threw up.'

'I saw that,' Bob said. 'How old was you, Corcho?'

'Seventeen. I threw up on myself. I can still remember that one. But he was one of those crazy ones. He even carried two guns.'

'You?' Billy said. 'But you're supposed to be fast.'

'He is, boy,' Bob said. 'He is. He got that way. You got to be good and you got to be lucky to live long enough to get as good as Corcho.'

'Or you, Bob,' I said, 'or you.'

He grinned and he sure didn't look seventy. 'Cup of coffee, Corcho?'

'Sure, Bob.'

'Boy?' Billy didn't say anything. 'I mean in a cup this time.'

'Sure, Sheriff Hollinger. Corcho, I mean Mr. Bliss, were you really as fast as the Deacon?'

'Kid,' I said, 'I'm just as fast as he *was*. Would you like to be just as fast as I *was*?'

He didn't even hear me. 'We can break out,' he said. 'I already got a plan.'

'You been smoking *mota*? You are moon-high loco. You are in for twenty-four hours. Just a day. Besides that, you backshot a good friend of mine. If I had a gun, I'd shoot you right now.'

'Come on, Mr. Bliss. I didn't know he was your friend and I don't care about the twenty-four hours. I'll help you and we'll slip over into Mexico. Say,' he dropped his voice, 'did you ever hear about Lara's secret treasure? You and me, we could – '

Before he could finish, the door swung open. Bob had the coffeepot in his right hand but his gun was out before the pot hit the floor. It was the red-headed lieutenant and the skinny deputy.

The lieutenant yelled, 'Barricade yourself. The revolutionaries are attacking Birdwell, up the river. Just came in on the telegraph.'

'No hold on,' Bob said.

'They need every man they can get. A citizens' posse is leaving now.' The deputy ran back out.

'A citizens' posse? Not without me,' Bob roared. 'Deputy!'

The skinny deputy ran back in. He had one spur on and one in his hand.

'Guard the prisoners. Don't let them kill each other and do not *ever* get near the cell doors. No matter what!'

'But, Sheriff, there's a posse on the way – '

'And I'm leading it.' He picked a Winchester off the rack

and stuck two boxes of shells in his coat pocket. He ran out. We could hear horses and men for about five minutes. Then it was too quiet.

The deputy felt it and was bolting the door when Pinkerton came in. The deputy felt a whole lot better. 'Missed the fighting.' He was about Billy's age. 'I could do a lot better than the old man if I ever got a chance. I shoot better and I'm a whole lot younger. I can get off six shots in less than two seconds,' he said.

'Let me see your side arm.' Pinkerton held his hand out.

'What?'

'Your revolver.'

Pinkerton took it, turned the cylinder, punched out a shell and then let the hammer fall on an empty cylinder. 'Maybe you won't shoot yourself,' he said.

Pinkerton took down a double-barreled sawed-off shotgun. He checked the loads.

'Double aught?' I asked.

'Double aught. Nine marble-sized holes in the belly, Corcho.'

'I know.'

'Don't try to scare us,' Billy said.

'Us?' Pinkerton cocked his head at me.

'Him,' I said, 'he don't scare. Me, yes.'

'Listen,' the deputy said, 'the cavalry's back already.' He reached for the big crossbar.

'No,' Pinkerton said, 'leave it.'

'But . . . '

Pinkerton looked out the curtained window. 'Lights out,' he snapped. When he turned to whisper, his face was chalk-white. 'Mexican bandits.'

'*Revolucionarios*,' I said automatically.

'They with you?' he asked.

I laughed. It was too much.

Pinkerton said, 'Maybe you really are crazy.' He pointed both barrels at the door. 'I'll take the door, deputy. You take the window.'

Then Lara's big voice boomed out. 'Corcho, you *cabrón*.

I know you're in there. Come on out. Come on out or we'll blast you out. I got some dynamite,' he added.

'He wants me. If I don't come out, he's going to dynamite the jail.'

Pinkerton looked at the deputy.

'He's right,' the deputy said, 'and that's Lara hisself.'

'Himself,' I said. 'Why don't you try to speak properly?' I started laughing again. I guess Pinkerton was close to being right about me being crazy.

'Send one man in,' Pinkerton yelled, 'and we'll discuss terms.'

The deputy took his revolver out and threw it on the floor.

'Billy,' Pinkerton said, 'you want to help? I'll let you out. Get you a gun.'

'Lara?' Billy said. 'Hell, no. I'm a prisoner.' He spoke to me. 'And it serves you right, you son of a bitch. You deserve to die. Making fun of me. Sure I killed your buddy. And I almost got you. Gunfighter. Old broken-down liar!'

'He says "no"!' I said to Pinkerton.

'For God's sake, let him go,' the deputy said.

'You might as well,' I said. It didn't much matter to me.

'We're ready to light the dynamite,' Lara said.

'Open the door,' the Pinkerton said.

Of course not just the one man came in. Two booted captains came in first, then Lara.

Pinkerton pointed the shotgun at me.

'You try to take him, I'll kill him first.'

Lara looked surprised. 'Go ahead,' he said.

The deputy had to translate that three times before the Pinkerton got it.

'You mean he doesn't care? But tell him the man's going to hang for murder.'

Lara thought that was funny. 'No, he was one of my men. They don't desert, and if they do, *I* shoot them.'

'Then shoot him,' Billy yelled.

'No,' Lara said, 'we don't want to shoot my old *compañero* Corcho. Anyway, not here. You want to shoot him, shoot.'

Pinkerton was holding that double barrel on me, but he had three shot guns pointing at his back.

'Kill him,' Billy yelled.

Lara glanced at the kid, then back to the Pinkerton agent. He said, 'Either shoot him, or let him go. But now!'

There was no mistake in Lara's tone. He was no bluffer.

'Go ahead, Pinkerton,' I said. I thought I knew what Lara had in mind and I thought that I'd rather go a little quicker. I was sick. Stomach about to let go. Always the same before a fight. Except this time there would not even be the heat of a fight. Just a load of buckshot, if I was lucky.

'Let Lara have him, Pinkerton. I'll donate my five hundred.'

Lara wanted to know what Billy said and nodded thoughtfully when the deputy translated.

'Well?' Lara said.

'Here goes nine thousand dollars,' The Pinkerton said and broke the shotgun open. He extracted the shells and put the gun in the rack.

'The other one, too,' Lara said. He didn't miss much. Pinkerton took the short-barreled .38 and put it with the shotgun.

'So long, Corcho.' Billy laughed. 'I guess I'll never get a chance to show you some real gun work.'

'What did the boy say?' Lara asked.

I told him.

'Why is he so mad?'

'It would take too long,' I told him.

'You don't like this *gringo cabrón*, eh?'

'No. He killed a friend. I don't get to like people who do that. You know!'

'Yes,' Lara said, 'I know. Poor Pablo.' He picked up the Pinkerton's pistol. 'Who'd he kill?' He pointed at Billy.

'Romero. Lieutenant Romero. He was a deserter,' I added.

'Sure,' Lara said. 'He was a deserter. I would have shot him.'

One of the captain's found the keys. They let me out. Then Lara said, 'Him, too.'

'Why him?' I asked.

'You're a very good man with guns. Better, maybe, than Pablo. Let's see how good the little boy is.'

Billy understood. They had to drag him out of the cell. They took the deputy's gun and holster and buckled it around Billy. Lara unbuckled his gun belt and strapped it on me. He checked the loads and took out four. 'I'm leaving you the one,' he said.

Pinkerton said, 'This is illegal. Dueling carries a murder charge.'

Lara motioned to a cell. They threw a blanket over Pinkerton's head and tied him in it. The deputy was face down on the floor. He had his hands over his ears. I could understand how he felt. If they killed him, he didn't want to know anything until the bullet let the black in.

'Okay,' Lara said. '*Adelante, muchachos.*'

'What'd he say?' Billy asked.

He knew as well as I did but I told him. 'He says go ahead. Draw. I'll give you the first chance.'

Billy wasn't about to draw, but then I didn't care. Lara was probably going to injun me around with cactus spines through my balls and cut my eyelids off so I could see the sun better while red ants crawled and stung, with maybe a little fire around my toes to keep me from being bored. I wanted Billy to draw and shoot. If he missed, I'd shoot Lara, maybe I'd shoot him anyway.

'Come on, Billy boy,' I said.

'If I wanted to, I'd draw and shoot while you're thinking about it. Go on, draw.'

Lara asked me what all the chatter was about but one of the captains spoke up.

'The big one tells the little one to draw first. That big one, he's got balls.'

'Thanks,' I said. 'Well, kid?'

'It's not fair,' he said. 'Not all of you. I'll meet you anywhere you like alone. But not with your gang.'

'*My* gang!'

'He won't draw?' Lara asked.

'No,' the captain said.

Lara shot him as casually as he'd flick his horse with a quirt. Then I drew. Lara was looking into the barrel. He grinned.

'You are better than Pablo. At some things.'

'You'll be dead,' I said. 'I'm going anyway and you and I will ride a ways together or we'll both go to hell right here and now.'

Lara swung the gun barrel my way. I pulled the trigger. There was a click.

'Lara,' I said, 'you are a pure no-good son of a whore.'

Lara laughed and laughed. Tears came to his eyes. 'Come along,' he said. 'Come on, *hombre*, I'm not going to kill you. You're going to take Pablo's place.'

I stopped in the doorway. 'You want me to take Pablo's place?'

'Sure. I make you my top *coronel*. You get Pablo's pay' – he crossed himself – 'and you will get his rank. You are a smart *cabrón* and I need someone. We got to drive these *pinches* Federalistas out of the North.'

'You want me to take Pablo's place.' I kept repeating it as we rode towards the bridge. There were no shots, no American soldiers. Just Lara, maybe thirty ragged *revolucionarios* and me.

Lara read my mind. 'They're up at Birdwell chasing me,' he said.

I reined up at the river. 'I don't shoot prisoners like Pablo did!'

'That was not good,' Lara said. 'We can use new men. We can teach them to be good soldiers. If the *cabrones* don't learn, then we shoot them!'

I nodded and we rode on a bit. I knew what the rebels were up against and I guess maybe there were a lot of things that could be a whole lot better. Maybe Lara meant well.

I reined in again. 'You serious?'

'*Sí*, Coronel Bliss, I am serious.' Somehow I knew he was.

'How about the tower? I get my cut.'

Lara reined in. He motioned the others ahead. He said quietly, 'You can have it all. These men, some of them, they won't fight if there is not any loot. The money we get we buy guns and bullets. There is never enough. Once in a while, Pablo and me – ' He stopped. 'Now, you and me, we take some mules and we load them with rocks and we hide them in the tower. I was a bandit and a *chingón* of a bandit, but now I'm a general and a *chingón* of a general and you and me we'll drive these *pinches* Federalistas out of Chihuahua.'

'General,' I said, 'that was quite a speech.'

'You get a *soldadera*, you know, a woman that goes along with you, too,' he said.

'Yeah, I'd like that. Is Carmencita around?'

'I married her, you *cabrón*,' he said.

A high angry voice startled my horse and a rider came out of the darkness. 'Oh, no,' I groaned. 'No! It can't be. Not just now!'

But it was. Pearl spurred up alongside me and whacked me with her quirt.

'Camencita, huh?' She whacked me again and I put the spurs to my horse and let out a Mexican yell.

'*¡Viva mi General Lara!*' I yelled. '*¡Viva le recolución! ¡Viva mi querida Pearl!* Come on, honey,' I said, and the whole bunch of us stampeded across the river into Mexico yipping and laughing, Pearl right behind me.

ALSO AVAILABLE IN CORONET BOOKS

LOUIS L'AMOUR

☐	02460 7	To Tame A Land	35p
☐	01022 3	Hondo	25p
☐	02775 4	The Tall Stranger	35p
☐	02708 8	Heller With A Gun	35p
☐	02409 7	Last Stand At Papago Wells	35p

THORNE DOUGLAS

☐	18876 6	The Big Drive	35p

FRANK WYNNE

☐	18515 5	Sweeny's Honour	30p
☐	18295 4	Gundown	30p

WILLIAM RAYNER

☐	19487 1	Bloody Affray At Riverside Drive	35p

All these books are available at your bookshop or newsagent, or can be ordered direct from the publisher. Just tick the titles you want and fill in the form below.

CORONET BOOKS, P.O. Box 11, Falmouth, Cornwall.

Please send cheque or postal order. No currency, and allow the following for postage and packing:

1 book – 10p, 2 books – 15p, 3 books – 20p, 4-5 books – 25p, 6-9 books – 4p per copy, 10–15 books – 2½p per copy, over 30 books free within the U.K.

Overseas – please allow 10p for the first book and 5p per copy for each additional book.

Name ....

Address ....

....